THIRTEEN, FOURTEEN... LITTLE BOY UNSEEN

REBEKKA FRANCK BOOK 7

WILLOW ROSE

Copyright Willow Rose 2015
Published by Jan Sigetty Boeje
All rights reserved.

No part of this book may be reproduced, scanned, or distributed in any printed or electronic form without permission from the author.

This is a work of fiction. Any resemblance of characters to actual persons, living or dead is purely coincidental. The Author holds exclusive rights to this work. Unauthorized duplication is prohibited.

Special thanks to my editor Jean Pacillo
http://www.ebookeditingpro.com

Cover design by Juan Villar Padron,
https://juanjjpadron.wixsite.com/juanpadron

Follow Willow Rose on BookBub:
https://www.bookbub.com/authors/willow-rose

Connect with Willow Rose:
willow-rose.net

To Camilla.

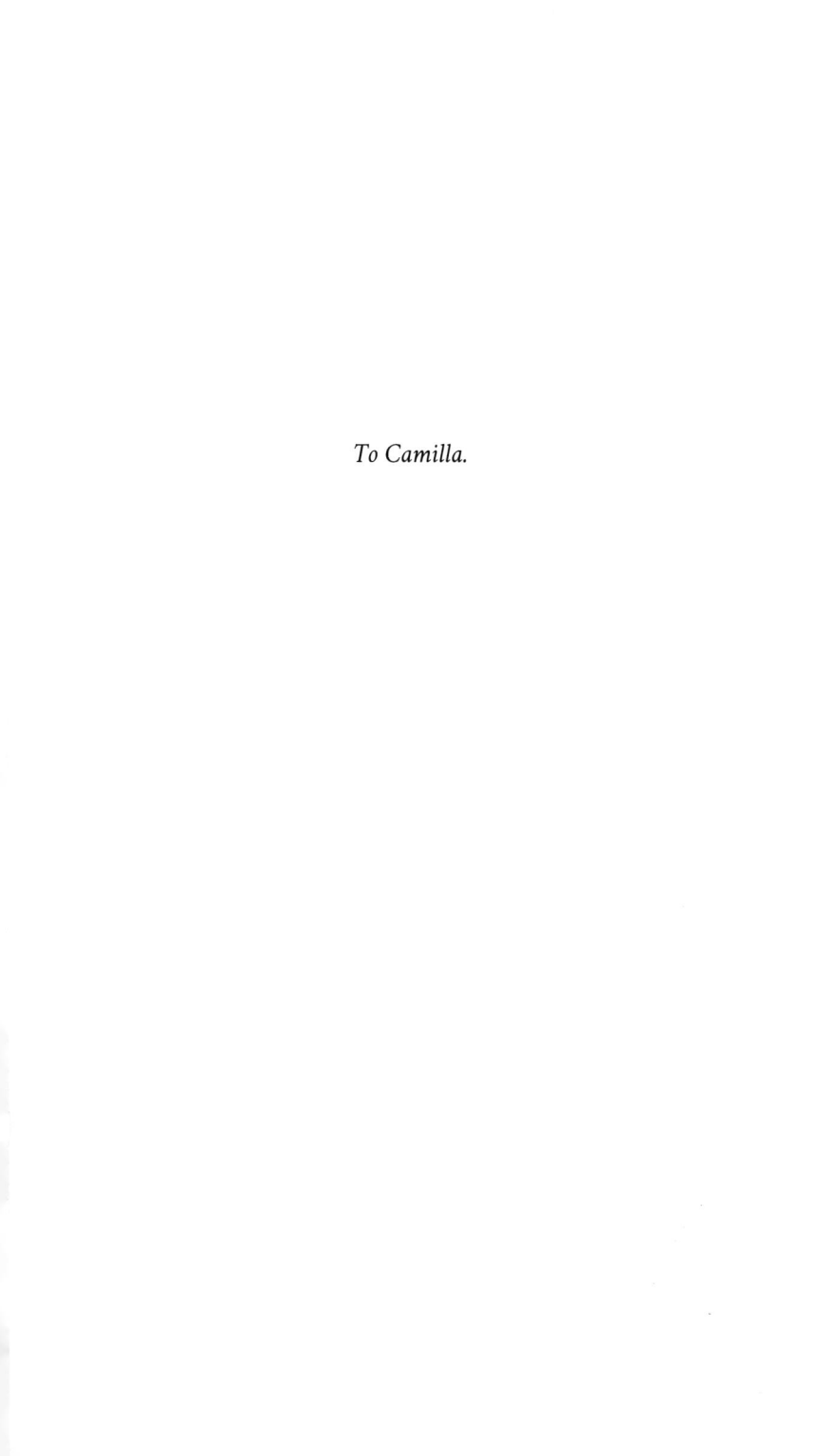

PROLOGUE

At first, nine-year old Steffen thought it was an animal. That it was some sort of sea creature surfacing from its cave underneath the black water. It made no sound as it broke through the still surface.

As usual on weekends, Steffen was playing by the lake on his grandmother's farm outside of Karrebaeksminde. It was early afternoon on a beautiful Sunday in January, the last day of Christmas break. It was one of those clear days where you could see your own breath, and the wind bit his cheeks.

He had brought Bastian, his grandmother's dog to the lake with him, and soon the dog started barking, upon discovering the massive lumps rocking in the water. Steffen stood like he was frozen and stared at the two big chunks. He didn't realize he had stopped breathing. Steffen finally took in a deep gasping breath. His heart was racing in his chest, just like the time when his grandfather had told him the story of the man who had stolen children and buried them in the forest behind their farm many years ago. Only this was worse.

This was a lot worse.

Bastian kept barking and was moving closer to the water. Steffen wondered what to do. The water was black as coal. The lumps were floating in the middle of the lake. Should he swim out to them? His grandparents had always warned him about the lake.

"It's bottomless," his grandmother would say, with those big worried eyes of hers. "Don't go too close, and certainly don't jump in. You'll never be able to get out again, you hear me?"

Steffen had heard her every time, and he feared the lake even more than he feared the tall slim man that his grandfather told him lived in the forest and kidnapped children.

"I don't know what to do, Bastian," he said.

He wanted so badly to know what it was that was floating around out there. It could be one or maybe two of those manatees that he had seen at the zoo. It kind of looked like them. Except these seemed to be wearing clothes and to have hair. Did manatees have hair? Steffen didn't think so. But, again, he had only seen one in the zoo.

Curiosity bit at his stomach. He wanted so badly to get closer.

Steffen took another step towards the lake, feeling how his wellies sank into the soft mud surrounding it. He gasped, remembering his grandmother's words, then stepped backwards. His wellies made a popping sound when he pulled them out of the mud. He grabbed a long stick and tried to poke the animal, but it didn't move. He poked it again, harder, but this time the stick went through the skin. Steffen gasped and let go of the stick, which remained inside the skin hole. There was no blood where the stick had poked through.

Many thoughts ran through the boy's mind as he looked at

the floating mass. He wondered if it could be zombies emerging to take over the world. The thought was scarier than anything else he could think of.

He was beyond terrified of zombies.

Steffen stared and gasped for air for a few moments longer, while imagining the two zombies lifting their heads and climbing out of the water. Then, he finally turned around and ran, Bastian running right behind him. His legs were burning as he sprinted across the fields, where he had so many fond memories of him helping his grandfather harvest the potatoes in the early summertime. He ran for his life, not daring to turn and look back to see if the zombies had taken up the pursuit. His mind was filled with images from that *World War Z* movie his older brother had let him watch once when they were home alone. He knew that zombies could run. He knew that zombies were fast.

There was no time to waste.

1

He remembered everything about her. The man remembered every single little detail. Her long black hair, the birthmark next to her nose that was the same as his own, the way she moved her pointer finger when she explained something, and the way she was careful to only show the tips of her teeth when smiling, because she didn't like the way her gums showed if she smiled all the way. He remembered all that and so much more and thought about it every day, especially when he looked at his own reflection.

But what he missed the most and what he feared forgetting, was her laughter. That light joyful sound of her being happy. It had been many years since he had last heard that sound, and even if he imagined her from time to time standing right in front of him, imagined her talking to him, he could never recreate the sound of her laughter.

He closed his eyes and imagined he was with her, playing in their backyard. When he dreamed about them, they were always young children, four or five years old, playing on the swing set that their dad had built for them.

Those were the happy days.

Their parents' life together had started with such promise. They grew up on farms near each other and met when their mother was just eighteen and their father nineteen. Their mother was an exceptionally pretty brunette, and had spent much of her teens fighting off guys who were too fresh. Their father, a tall, shy black-haired man, was different. When their parents used to talk of how they met, their mother would light up and shake her head, while saying with sparkling eyes, "Your father asked me to dance, and at first I thought *the good part is, he's not too handsome.*"

Three years later, they married and moved to a nearby city. Their mother used to tell people how happy their father had been upon learning that he was going to be the father of twins, and his euphoria when they were born on May 22nd 1986.

The man remembered how his mother would talk about the time of their birth. How she would tell the same story over and over again about their father.

"The nurse asked him, *is it boys or girls?*" his mother would say with such a joyful laughter in her voice. "And he said, *I don't know! I just know there's two of them!*"

At this point in the story, everyone would laugh. Even those that had heard it before. It was a great and heart-warming story.

Shortly after their birth, their father had been promoted to partner at his law firm and they had bought a house in Karrebaeksminde, only a fifteen minute drive from the firm's office in Naestved. It was a small town where they could get a beautiful house by Smaalandsfarvandet, where all the rich people lived or had summer residences if they lived in Copenhagen.

Soon, their father became a very respected lawyer who worked for many wealthy clients, while his wife took care of the twins at home, something she considered a privilege. They were happy and at the peak of their life.

The man opened his eyes and looked at his own reflection in the mirror of his bathroom again. Sadness came over him as it always did when he took these trips down memory lane. His mother had told most of it to him, especially how it had been in their younger years, but some he remembered, some small parts he remembered vividly, and was often haunted by those parts in dreams.

He bent over and turned on the faucet. He splashed water onto his face, and then wiped it with a towel. He touched his cheeks gently and felt his beard. It had taken awhile to grow it, but he finally seemed to have succeeded. But that also meant his hair was thinning on top, just like it had done to his dad when he had been that age. It was the course of nature when you were a man, and there was no way to avoid it.

It's no use fighting who you are, his father had always said. *You get what you get and you make the best of it.*

The man didn't like to remember his childhood, but on certain days he couldn't help himself. Like today…when it was their birthday. But it wasn't time for him to dwell on sad memories now. He sighed and looked at himself in the mirror while getting dressed. He liked the way he looked in the uniform.

"You would have loved me in this, Alex" he said to his own reflection.

He put his badge on his belt and took his gun from the top drawer. He looked at himself holding the gun in the mirror, and then smiled.

"If only you could see me now, Alex. You would be so proud. This is all for you, you know."

The man smiled again, then pretended to shoot the dresser next to him, making the gun's noise with his mouth like he used to when playing policeman as a child. Alex had loved to play cops and robbers. It had been her favorite game when they were children.

But it's not a game anymore. No this is serious. D-e-a-d-ly serious!

The man grinned, then put the gun in the holster and corrected his hat to make sure it was straight. He grabbed the car keys from the table by the door, and with the address of his next victim in his hand, he left the house.

2

"Welcome back. How was your Christmas?"

Sara looked like she had been sitting in the same spot all through Christmas break. She was in the exact same place as I had left her two weeks earlier. She was even wearing the same dress and black stockings. The pastry sitting in front of her seemed new, though.

I walked to my desk and put down my laptop. "Great. It was really nice to have a break from things," I said, and took off my jacket.

The office was a mess, but I didn't care. I had chosen to take the two weeks off when the kids were out from school. Sara had taken care of the office while I was gone. I smiled and looked at her as I pulled out my chair and sat down. She smiled back. Her red hair was messier than usual. Somewhere in there, a butterfly hairpiece had gotten lost, and I could see a part of it that was sticking out.

"How were things here at the office while I was gone?" I asked.

She shrugged and slurped her coffee. "Quiet, I guess. Plenty of drunk drivers on the scanner, a burglar got caught yesterday, and someone stole a boat at the marina two days ago, but other than that, pretty quiet."

"That's good."

I got up and went into the small kitchen and poured myself a cup. I was tired. Since the accident in October where I had been trapped underground in a sinkhole, my sleep had been difficult. I had constant nightmares and had been very edgy, jumping at the smallest sounds, or even worse…getting anxiety attacks when left alone. Those were the worst times, when everything went quiet. I couldn't stand it. I needed people around me, and I needed there to be noise, ordinary noise, like traffic. Oh, how I had started to love traffic. And nature. I loved driving outside of town and just walking in the forest or along the beach, or just stopping the car and taking a walk in a field. The open spaces and the blue sky were my rescue. I craved them constantly.

Sune had been great through most of it the last couple of months. But I got the feeling he didn't quite understand how I felt. Of course he didn't. How could he?

I grabbed my coffee and went back to my desk. Work made me forget and not think of being trapped. I looked at my face briefly in the mirror as I passed it and sighed. I was still very skinny and hadn't gained much of the weight I had lost while trapped underground. I hadn't had much appetite and had to force myself to eat. It was hard when you didn't feel good. I had this sense of anxiety constantly lingering in my stomach, that urgent feeling, a slight panic that came over me from time to time. The smallest noise would make me jump. I woke at night with a fast beating heart and simply had to run outside, just to make sure the sky was still there. Just to breathe the fresh air. Sune seemed to understood most of it, he understood why I was scared, why I had these attacks, but he had a hard time understanding how long it took for me to get rid of the feelings. Some days I ate a lot. I would stuff my face in fear of never seeing food again, but then it would be too much for my body, and I would feel sick for days afterwards and hardly eat anything. It was like there was no middle ground.

"So, what's on for today?" Sara asked, when I returned to my desk.

"As a matter of fact, I don't know," I said. "I haven't heard from Jens-Ole yet. I'm expecting his call any moment now, when they're done with the morning meeting at headquarters. While I spoke, the phone on my desk started ringing. I could tell by the aggressive sound that it had to be him.

I chuckled.

"As we speak of the…"

Sara laughed. "That sure sounds like him."

"Rebekka!" Jens-Ole yelled into the other end. I smiled at the sound of his voice. As always, he sounded like it was of top urgency. I liked that about him. There was never a dull moment.

"Yes, dear. And a happy New Year to you as well. What do you have for me today?"

He grumbled something sounding slightly like *happy New Year*, but I wasn't sure.

"Bodies," he said. "Two bodies. Husband and wife. Found yesterday in a lake not far from Karrebaeksminde by some boy and his dog. I want them in my paper! If the dog is cute, I want a big photo on the front page!"

3

SUNE WAS CALLED in and met me by my car that I had parked in the street in front of the office. Jens-Ole had emailed me the details. Sune and I shared a quick kiss before we drove off.

"Was my dad up when you left?" I asked.

"Yes."

"Good," I said. I was worried about him. He was getting weaker and weaker as the days passed. We had gotten help from the county, and a nurse came every day to take care of him while we were at work.

My father had developed a tendency to stay in bed most of the day. He needed to get up and get moving, the doctor had told us. He was losing his muscle mass too quickly and that was a slippery slope, according to the doctor. It made it harder and harder for my dad to get out of bed, with the result that he only lost more muscle. He simply had to get out of bed every day and get his body moving and his blood pumping. "So, what do we know about the bodies?" Sune asked.

"I called the forensics team a few minutes ago," I said, and took a right turn as we got to the city limit. "They haven't identified them yet, but they are a male and a female, about forty-five to fifty years old. The police believe they must have drowned; that they went fishing and the boat sank. They've been in the water a long time. Several weeks, they think. Maybe even months."

"How come they weren't found before?" Sune asked, as I found the road leading towards Naestved. We were in the countryside now, and the houses were few. Horses in a paddock were wearing covers. Frost had painted the grass white.

"It's been a rough winter so far. The water has been cold, and they think that's why it has taken so long for the bodies to resurface. They were found floating face down. I don't know how much you know about these things, but a cadaver in the water starts to sink as soon as the air in its lungs is replaced with water. Once submerged, the body stays underwater until the bacteria in the gut and chest cavity produce enough methane gas, hydrogen sulfide, and carbon dioxide to float it to the surface like a balloon. But the buildup of methane, hydrogen sulfide, and other gases can take days or weeks, depending on the temperature."

"I see. So, it was the boy who found the bodies floating in the lake?" Sune asked.

"Yes. They can have been there for quite awhile. But our part is simply to tell about the find. It's as easy as can be. I say we simply interview the boy and get his picture. I spoke to his mother earlier, and they've kept him home from school today, since he was in a great shock from the find yesterday. He's at his grandparents' place, and they have the dog there with them. Jens-Ole is very keen on getting the dog in the paper, for some reason. He thinks cute animals sell newspapers."

Sune leaned his seat back with a sigh and a smile. "That shouldn't be too hard. All dogs are cute."

I chuckled while the GPS on my phone told me we had to

make a left turn down a small dirt road. I blinked and turned, and we bumped towards the small farmhouse behind tall trees. A pit-bull bull ran towards us as I parked the car in front of the main building.

I looked at Sune, who seemed terrified. The dog stared at us with its almost white eyes.

"I sure hope that's not the dog," Sune said. "Please tell me that isn't the dog."

I couldn't help laughing. Of course, Jens-Ole had thought it was this little cute dog with big brown puppy-dog eyes that he could put on the front cover and sell a lot of newspapers.

"Maybe we can Photoshop it?" I asked.

Sune shuddered while the dog barked outside our window. It stared at us, looking vicious.

"I think we need a lot more than Photoshop here," he grumbled.

An elderly woman came out from the house and started yelling at the dog to get away from the car. She shooed it away, and we could finally get out.

I shook the woman's hand.

"Rebekka Franck, *Zeeland Times*," I said. "This is my photographer, Sune Johansen."

The woman smiled gently and nodded, when I spotted a small boy in the opening of the door. The grandmother saw him too as she turned her head.

"Let's go inside," she said. "Steffen prefers to stay in the house these days. Says he's afraid of zombies, the poor thing."

4

WE GOT BACK to the office just before lunch. Sune and I had picked up sandwiches for everyone on our way, which we ate before I started writing the article about Steffen and Bastian, who found two bodies in the lake. It wasn't a big story, and I knew it wouldn't reach the front cover. Sune did his best to find a picture where the dog looked slightly less malicious, but it still wasn't front-page material. Not in the way Jens-Ole wanted it to be.

I wrote a couple of small articles about a new bakery opening on our main street and one about one of Karrebaeksminde's beloved citizens who would turn one hundred tomorrow. I sent it all, along with Sune's pictures, and looked at the clock. It was time for us to pick up Tobias and Julie from school. When we were about to leave, I still hadn't heard from Jens-Ole, who needed to approve my articles in case he had any last minute changes.

"I can go get the kids alone, if you like," Sune said.

"Nah, I want to go home anyway. I'll just have to make the changes at home, in case he has any," I said.

I grabbed my laptop from the desk, knowing very well that

Jens-Ole wouldn't be too happy with the article where the boy spoke about zombies and how he thought they would come after him, and a dog so snappy-looking I wasn't even sure he was going to print the picture. Well, it wasn't my problem, was it? I had done my part, and now I wanted to go home.

We picked up William first at his day-care. His day-care mom, Anette, was a woman who took care of five kids in her own home, and he absolutely adored her. We all did. It was good to know that he was being well taken care of while we worked. My dad had gotten too sick to take care of him, so it was the best solution for all. William smiled widely and stumbled insecurely towards us when we entered Anette's house. In his eagerness to get to us, he fell to his knees and burst into a loud scream. I hurried towards him and picked him up. The feeling of defeat wouldn't go away, and he continued crying as we carried him to the car. I felt a knot in my stomach while trying to comfort him. It was the guilt nagging me. Even though I knew he was in a good place, I still felt bad for working instead of taking care of him at home. It was silly, really. The kid was almost two years old.

"He loves it at Anette's," Sune said, as we got into the car and I had strapped William in the seat. "It's good for him to get out and be with other children," he continued.

I started the car with a sigh. "I know. I just feel so guilty for wanting a career. That's all."

"I know you do, but you've got to let it go. If you stayed at home, you would go nuts. You're simply not cut out for the stay-at-home-mom life. You have to acknowledge that and make peace with it. You like your job, and there is nothing wrong with that."

"It's just so hard," I grumbled. "Especially since the sinkhole-incident. I can't stop thinking about how I need to cherish every moment I have with him, how I don't want to miss one second of his life."

Sune leaned over and kissed me. "You just need to let it go," he whispered. "That's all."

I looked into his eyes with a strange feeling. I knew what he was saying, but I wasn't sure I agreed. Not anymore. I wasn't sure I wanted to let it go. Something had changed inside of me, and I had no idea how to embrace it. I had started thinking a lot more about life and how I spent my time, how precious every little moment really was. I wasn't sure Sune fully understood the extent of it. It wasn't just some cliché for me anymore. I wasn't a kitty-poster on Facebook with a message.

I backed out of the parking lot in front of Anette's house. Anette was standing in the window with the two other kids that hadn't been picked up yet, waving at William. I waved at her.

"Look William! Anette!" I said and pointed.

William forgot all about being sad and waved eagerly, while chewing his pacifier greedily.

"Let's go get Tobias and Julie," I said.

William shrieked with joy. He could hardly contain his excitement, and both his arms and legs moved as he yelled, "Tobby...Juju!"

5

Jens-Ole wasn't too thrilled about the article and decided to drop it to page seven. He would print the picture, but not in a big size, he told me on the phone, as soon as we came in the door. The big kids were tired and sat on the couch, each with an iPad in hand, playing Minecraft, while William wouldn't leave my shoulder and clung to me like he wasn't sure he was going to ever see me again.

"Other than that, your articles were all fine. No need to correct anything," Jens-Ole said, to my relief. I really didn't want to spend my evening rewriting an article I wasn't too fond of in the first place.

"Tomorrow is a new day," Jens-Ole said. "Maybe you've already gotten your nose into a story?"

Usually, I would have done just that. It never took me many minutes back on the job before I had lots of stories I wanted to research, but for the first time, I really didn't have anything. It kind of surprised me, and I didn't want to admit it. Instead, I lied.

"I have a few things I'd like to look into," I said, while

William was fussing in my arms, trying to grab the phone out of my hand.

"That's my girl. Can't wait to hear more tomorrow," Jens-Ole said, right before we hung up.

I put the phone in my pocket, wondering if I could come up with a good story by morning. I shrugged. I had been through this before. A lot could happen overnight. Maybe something would come up.

Julie and Tobias were suddenly fighting, and Julie was screaming.

"Hey! What's going on in here?" I yelled, and stormed into the living room.

"Tobias pulled my hair!" Julie said, crying.

Sune came up behind me.

"Don't pull her hair! Say you're sorry," I said angrily.

William was crying in my arms as well now. He was angry because I didn't let him have the phone.

Julie looked at Tobias, waiting for her apology. It didn't come.

"See, he doesn't even want to say he's sorry," she said and looked at me. "He's so mean."

"Am not!" Tobias argued.

"Oh, yes you are. You're always so mean to me!"

"Just say you're sorry, for crying out loud," I said.

"Hey, hey, not so fast," Sune said, and stepped forward. "Who says he even did it?"

I looked at Sune. Was he for real? "Well, Julie said he did," I said.

"Maybe she's lying," Sune said.

"I'm not lying!" Julie said with a whining voice, and then started crying. "I'm NOT a liar!"

"No, of course you're not a liar," I said, trying to comfort her and William at the same time. "Sune didn't mean that."

"Yes, he did," Julie said. "He always thinks the worst of me."

"Oh, come on," Sune said. "Don't let her do this to you. She's such a drama queen." He looked at Tobias. "Did you do it, Tobias? Did you pull her hair?"

Tobias thought for a long time, then nodded.

"Ha!" Julie said. "Told you so."

"Okay, well now that we've established that he did pull her hair, maybe now he can say he is sorry?" I said to Sune. The tension between us was getting bad. I didn't like it. There was nothing like our children that could make us turn on each other lately. It was becoming a bad habit. But, I had to defend my child, didn't I?

"Maybe there's a reason why he pulled her hair," Sune said. "Tobias doesn't do anything like this without a reason."

We all looked at Tobias to get an explanation. "She stole everything in my chest and won't give it back," he said.

"Chest?" I asked.

"In Minecraft," Sune said, annoyed, like I was supposed to know what they were talking about. "They put all the stuff they gather in their chests."

"Did you steal all of his stuff?" I asked Julie.

"He took my diamond that I found. So, I stole everything he had," she answered. I looked at Tobias. My head was starting to hurt.

"You didn't find it. I found it first!" Tobias said.

I looked at Sune, thinking I was ready to let them handle this on their own. I was getting tired of the discussion, but Sune wouldn't let it go.

"You can't just steal everything, Julie," he said.

I stared at him with surprise. "Hey, don't take it out on her," I said. "It seems to me, they were both in on it. Besides, I think it's slightly worse to pull someone's hair than to steal some things in a computer game."

Sune looked at me like I was an idiot. "How can you say

that? If she hadn't stolen the things, Tobias never would have touched her."

"I still don't think…" I didn't finish the sentence before the doorbell rang. Sune didn't look like he was ready to let go of the discussion, but I was happy to have an excuse to leave the room. I smiled at William and told him to never grow up before I opened the door.

Then, I froze.

"Hi, Rebekka."

It was David. David Busck.

6

"What are you doing here?" I asked, and hugged David tightly. I hadn't seen him since that day we got out of the limestone mine two and a half months ago. He had left the hospital before me and never said goodbye.

"I…I was in the neighborhood," David said, and looked at William. Loud arguing voices still came from the living room. "Is this a bad time?"

"No, no, come one in," I said, and pulled his arm.

"I could come again another time. I'm in town for a few days," he said, but I pulled him inside and closed the door.

"No way. You're staying for dinner," I said. "Sune! David is here, come say hello."

"David?" Sune came into the hallway. Then he smiled. It came off a little awkward, but I didn't think David noticed. I wondered why he was acting that way. They shook hands. "Hey…man…what are you doing here?"

"I was in town and thought I'd stop by to see how you were doing," he said, looking at me. Then he shrugged. "Anyway, you all seem to be well. I didn't mean to interrupt…"

"Nonsense," I interrupted him. "Stay for dinner."

It might not have been the best of decisions, but I just wanted to be friendly. David had been my friend and closest ally in the caves underground. I cared deeply for him and had long wondered how he was doing. But, I hadn't considered Sune's feelings in all this.

David sat in the kitchen while I cooked. I served him a glass of wine, while Sune stood in the doorway, looking like he couldn't decide whether to come in or stay out.

"So, how have you been?" I asked. "Why didn't you say goodbye at the hospital?"

I put the wine in front of David and he tasted it. "Well, I didn't want to disturb you," he said. "You were with your family."

"Still, you should have said goodbye," I said with a frown. "I've wondered for months what happened to you and where you went."

David chuckled. "It's nice to know," he said. "But, to be frank, it's been quite a journey. After I left the hospital, I went to Copenhagen, where I lived with a friend for awhile, trying to avoid the press."

"I know," I said. "The first weeks were brutal. They were constantly calling with the phone constantly ringing and the press even showing up on my doorstep. It's ironic to suddenly be on the other side of the microphone, huh? Well, you've tried it before, but it's a first for me."

"Can you believe those people who made deals with them?" David said.

"No! Lars Dalgas, the librarian! Who would have thought that he would end up a reality star?" I laughed.

David chuckled as well, and we went quiet for a little while, both thinking about Lars and the others trapped in the mines. The silence made Sune uncomfortable.

"So, what about that Lars?" he asked. "Why is it so funny that he is a reality star now?"

I shook my head and looked at David. Our eyes locked for a second. I turned my head. "It's not that funny. It's just that… well…" I shrugged. "I don't know how to explain it. Maybe it's not that funny after all."

I returned to peeling the potatoes in the sink. I felt bad for Sune. I could tell he felt left out, but I really didn't know how to explain Lars to him. I really didn't want to. A lot of things had happened down there that brought out the worst in people. It was better to be forgotten.

"No, I really want to know," Sune said with a slightly shrill voice. "Tell me everything about this Lars Dalgas."

I looked at David. "There really isn't much to tell…"

"Oh, then I must have gotten it all wrong then, 'cause a minute ago, it seemed like there was plenty to tell," Sune said.

David looked uncomfortable. He got up. "You know what? Thanks for the dinner invitation, but I need to take a rain check. I have stuff to do. I'll see you around, okay?" He shook Sune's hand, and then hugged me.

"But…" I tried.

"It's okay, Rebekka. I didn't mean to interrupt like this," he said, and almost ran out the door.

I was baffled.

Sune chuckled. "That was strange, huh?" he said with a laugh.

I stared at Sune. "What the hell was that?" I asked.

He looked like he didn't understand. "What do you mean?"

"Why did you, all of a sudden, act like this jealous boyfriend?"

"What do you mean?"

I rolled my eyes and returned to my potatoes. I felt sad that David had left so quickly. I really wanted to know how he had been. I had really missed him.

"Okay, so what if I got a little jealous, so what?" Sune said. I could tell by the sound of his voice that he wanted to fight.

"I really don't want to…" I said.

"I think you should. I think we need to talk about this," he said.

I turned and looked at him. His cheeks were red and his eyes wild. I didn't like him when he acted like this.

"Don't start…"

"Oh, I'll start whatever I need to," he said.

William started fussing in his high chair, where he was eating carrots and a banana.

"Let's begin with you explaining to me why you've been wondering about this guy for months?"

"What are you talking about?"

"You just said it yourself. You told him you had been wondering about him for months. Those were your words, not mine."

I exhaled. "I wondered about what had happened to him. Is that so strange? I care about people."

"So, now you care about him, do you?" Sune asked.

"Yes. Yes. I care about David. Is that so wrong? I mean, we went through a lot of stuff together in those caves; it's not something you simply forget after a few days. I'm never going to forget him or what happened to us."

Sune looked like I had offended him. "You'll never forget him? What does that mean? Did anything happen between you two down there? Why were you hugging him when we came down to rescue you?"

"What?" I grabbed William and got him out of his chair. He stumbled across the room.

"You two were standing awfully close when I entered that cave. In each other's arms even. I could tell something was going on between the two of you. I just knew it. I could tell by the way you looked at him. Don't you think I know you?" Sune was almost spitting when he spoke. I had never seen him like this.

"What do you mean?" I asked.

"How can you not know what I mean?? I walked in there, ready to rescue you, and then I found you...I find you in the arms of this...this...guy."

"Oh, my goodness. This has bothered you ever since, hasn't it? I can't even remember it."

"You don't remember that you were in his arms when I found you? You expect me to believe that?" Sune said.

I shook my head. "I...I really don't remember. I was starved and dehydrated. There's a lot from down there I don't remember."

Sune gritted his teeth.

"You don't believe me, do you?" I asked.

He shook his head. "No. I don't. There you have it. I can't stand the fact that you don't talk about what happened down there with...with him. Why won't you tell me about it?"

"Mostly because I only remember bits and pieces, but also because I really, really want to forget. I want to move on with my life. My life with you," I said, feeling tears pile up.

Sune bit his lip and shook his head. Julie and Tobias had started fighting again in the living room.

"I don't believe you. I think you want to remember. You wanted to when David stepped in the door, didn't you? You wanted to talk about old times and know *everything*," he said, making a mocking voice.

Julie started screaming again. I wiped my hands on a towel. "You know what? Believe what you want. I don't have time for this," I said, and walked into yet another war zone.

7

Pastor Klara Kemp was sitting in her office in the vicarage that belonged to Karrebaeksminde Church. She was working on her sermon for next Sunday, and thought with joy about last Sunday's speech. She had talked about gays and how homosexuality didn't belong in the church and how it was an abomination, according to the Bible. She had long watched where the country was going on this, and now that the church accepted *those kinds* of people getting married within the church walls, she knew it was time for her to speak up.

Pastor Kemp was old and knew she didn't have many years left before she had to resign. And she was determined to fight for the truth till the end. They'd have to carry her out of her church. She wasn't going to let anyone of *that kind* get married in her church. And she would let her congregation know how she felt about it. There was no doubt in her mind that she would never approve this.

When the head bishop had told her the church was ready to change its views on homosexuals and let them get married, she hadn't believed her own ears. She knew it was being debated. She knew there were forces of evil out there trying to change things, but she had never thought they would succeed.

"Never," she had replied when he told her this applied to her as well, that if a couple came to her and wanted her blessing and to be married in her church, she would have to do it.

"It says very clearly in Leviticus," she had continued. *"You shall not lie with a male as one lies with a female. It is an abomination."*

The Head Bishop had told her that this was the way it was going to be, no matter what she said. There was no way out of it. She had an obligation to do as she was told.

"Never," she now whispered into the small office in her vicarage, where she had lived for the past fifty years.

No, Pastor Kemp didn't like the way the church was going or how the devil had been allowed to darken everyone's mind and poison them with all this, making them believe they were just being open-minded and embracing the new.

"We shouldn't exclude anyone from the church," one of her colleagues had said a few years ago at a conference. "If God is love and two people love one another, who are we to judge? How can we tell them their love is not real? Isn't it between them and God? After all, we can't discriminate in the church. We're supposed to bring a message of love to the people."

Pastor Kemp had referred to the Bible and told him all homosexuals were sinners, and if they gave them their blessing, that would make them sinners as well. "You'll rot in hell," she told him, pointing at him with her cane. "All of you will. Mark my words."

But would they listen? Of course not. This entire country was going to burn in hell. She told them over and over again, whenever the newspapers came to her for a comment. They thought she was raving mad, but that didn't stop her. No one could. Not even her Head Bishop, who kept telling her that they would retire her. She didn't care.

So, last Sunday, Pastor Kemp had spoken to her congregation about it once again.

"There's a movement within the church that wants us to embrace homosexuals and bless them in our Lord's name. But, I tell you, they'll all rot in hell. It's Adam and Eve, not Adam and Steve," she had said, quoting one of the worst movies she had ever seen. Her own daughter, Camilla, had made her watch it many years ago, to make her understand her choice of lifestyle and how she was going to die. Pastor Kemp had watched *Philadelphia* over and over again after she put her daughter in the ground, after watching her wither away due to the gay-plague, due to her choices in life that ended up killing her. Just like her mother had told her they would. No, this atrocity had to be kept down. The opinions on this subject in the population were getting worse; people were accepting homosexuality and talking about it like it was the most normal thing in the world. With the result that more and more people were deceived into this…this lie…this *disease* from the pit of hell.

Pastor Kemp still remembered the day her daughter came to her and told her she was one of them. Told her she had a girlfriend. That she wanted to live her life in the worst sin possible. She had asked her to understand, asked her mother to bless them and what they called their relationship. She had asked her to open up her mind and told her this was the hardest thing she'd ever had to tell her mother, and that she had been terrified for years to let her know, because she knew how she felt about homosexuals.

Pastor Kemp hadn't cried that summer day in 1995. Not even when she told her to get out and never come back. Not when she looked into her daughter's eyes and told her she wasn't her daughter anymore. Not when her daughter cried and begged for her mother's acceptance.

But she did cry three years later, when Camilla came one day to the house holding a VHS-tape with the movie in her hand. Her face was pale and her body wasting away.

"I don't know how else to explain all this to you, Mom. But I hope this will," were the final words she ever said to her mother. Pastor Kemp watched the movie and that was when the tears started rolling across her cheeks. Three weeks later, Pastor Kemp received a call from the hospital in Copenhagen, telling her that her daughter was very sick and that it was time to say goodbye. Camilla hadn't been conscious and never knew that her mother sat beside her deathbed for three nights straight, crying and cursing the devil and all his lies. Knowing her daughter had lived her life in sin, that the devil had ruined her life and taken her with him to a place where she was burning up for eternity, was the worst part about this whole damn thing.

She knew then that fighting this disease would be the thorn in her side. Just like Paul's, she knew God would never take it away, and even if she asked him to remove it from her on a daily basis, she would have to struggle with it till the day she died.

Pastor Kemp hadn't yet finished writing next week's sermon when the doorbell interrupted her. She sighed and put down the pen. She looked at the old clock on the wall.

"Now, who would ring my doorbell at this hour?" she grumbled, annoyed. She was on a roll here, and really wanted to finish tonight. Who on earth would come to someone's house this late? Had people no manners anymore?

Thinking it could be someone who needed God's word for the night, she got up with much restraint and walked, leaning on her cane, towards the door. To make sure it was safe to open the door, she pulled the curtain to the side to see who it was, and spotted an officer outside in the streetlight.

"Yes?" she said, and opened the door, slightly irritated with being interrupted. She hid her irritation with a fake smile.

"What can I do for you, Officer?"

It wasn't until he took a step forward and she could see the officer's eyes that she realized that this time the devil had come for her.

"You?"

"Yes, Pastor. Me."

8

"What do you want?"

The man looked at the pastor with a smirk. He could tell she was afraid. He chuckled. He was holding his baton in one hand and letting it drop into the other with rhythmic movements.

The pastor looked at the baton with fear in her eyes. The man was enjoying this little display of power.

"Listen," she said with a pleading voice. "We only did what we thought was best for her…I never thought…"

Pastor Kemp stopped herself. She looked at the man while biting her lip. The man stared at the old woman, who was all of a sudden so humble. It was so unlike the pastor the man remembered from his childhood. The pastor that came to their house so often.

"You must fight this," he remembered her saying, her voice hissing like that of a cat when she spoke, sitting in their kitchen. "This kind of thing needs to be grabbed at an early age before it's too late. It's a lie from the devil, is what it is. It's a disease, and you need to cure her."

The man stared into the eyes of the pastor, those narrow

blue eyes staring right back at him. He scrutinized them, searching for a small sign of regret, just a little something telling him that she felt bad or was sorry for what they had done. But he saw none.

"I still believe it was for the best," she said.

The man chuckled. Of course she still believed that. Of course she had no idea how much pain she had inflicted upon the people around her. Of course she had no idea how much power she had and how she had misused that for so many years, making people's lives miserable. He had listened to her sermon last weekend, and he knew exactly how she felt. She hadn't changed since then. She didn't regret a single thing. There was no way of changing her attitude or her beliefs. But there was a way of making her pay for what she did.

The man lifted the baton and swung it at the old woman, striking her on the cheek. The blow made her fall backwards into the hallway of her house. She landed on the carpet with a loud thud.

She was still conscious when he stepped inside the house and closed the door behind him with a slam. She was still awake, just enough to look him in the eyes with a deep fear. It gave the man such great pleasure to see her beg for her life.

"Please," she sobbed.

The man lifted the baton again and slapped her on her chest. The woman moaned in pain. The sound made the man even more agitated, and he hit her again with great pleasure, while he heard the pastor's voice from back then in his parents' kitchen.

"You must train her. You must not let her give in to this. Pray over her every morning and every night. Pray that God will remove this sin from her life. Train her into understanding how wrong it is. And, if that doesn't work, you must do what is required."

That was when the pastor put a whip on the kitchen table.

From the crack in the kitchen door, where he was listening along with his sister, he remembered vividly seeing his mother stare at the whip, then back at the pastor.

"You can't be serious?" she said.

The pastor nodded. "I'm afraid I am. I think you need to be as well. You must do what it takes to make sure your daughter doesn't fall into sin. Whatever it takes, my child."

"Please, don't hurt me again," the pastor now moaned.

But the memory of the whip and what followed for years after for his sister removed any doubt the man might have had about his mission. He needed to make her pay for the anger she'd caused from hearing his sister scream in pain at night in the bunk bed underneath him, the anger from hearing her cry and the pain he would feel on his own burning skin when they dragged her to the bathroom and whipped her again and again. Didn't they know that when they hurt her, they hurt him as well? Being her twin, he felt every whiplash, every slap across her face, and even every humiliating word they used to try and make his sister change her ways.

He would never be able to forget.

"Please…" Blood was running from the old pastor's lip. It had spilled onto her white shirt.

"That's exactly what she said," he said, and lifted the baton once again. "That's exactly how she pleaded for her life when she was beaten again and again. Do you remember that? I bet you don't, old woman. But I do. I remember every scream, every plea and every night spent in pain. That's what I believe is hell. That is the hell I'm living in every day. Because of you, because of what you did. Now, there are many opinions of what hell really is. Will we burn for eternity? Will we be in pain? No one really knows, do they?"

The man chuckled and looked into the eyes of the old

pastor as he slammed the baton into her head so hard the light in her eyes went out. She stopped breathing immediately, and he leaned over and whispered in her ear, "But I guess you're about to find out."

9

"So, what have you got for me?"

Jens-Ole sounded like he was in a good mood.

I stared at the blank paper in front of me. I had been so busy with smoothing away conflicts at the house and trying to make things better between Sune and me that I had completely forgotten to try and find ideas. The morning at the house had been a nightmare, and I felt exhausted. I held my phone close to my ear, trying desperately to come up with something.

"Come on, Rebekka. Spit it out. I don't have all day," Jens-Ole said. "Got a newspaper to fill, remember?"

I stared, baffled, at the paper, then at the screen in front of me with yesterday's article of the boy and the dog. I had no idea what to say.

Just say something! Anything!

"Rebekka?"

I looked up. In front of me stood Sara. She handed me a small note. Then she smiled.

Who goes fishing in the winter? It said.

My eyes met hers. She shrugged. "Just a thought," she said,

and walked back to her desk.

I stared at the note, and then up at the article wherein I stated that it was a drowning accident. She was right. Sara was right. Something was off here. The lakes had been frozen for at least a month with the tough winter we had. The ice was hardly thick enough to walk on, anyone knew that. But still, they couldn't get a boat in the water. I stared at the note.

"Rebekka, are you still there?" Jens-Ole said.

"Who goes fishing in the winter?" I asked.

"What? I don't know. Lots of people, I guess. What are you talking about?"

"Only hardcore sports fishing men, the way I see it. And they would have to be dressed for it, right?"

"What on earth are you talking about, Rebekka? Fill me in here," Jens-Ole said.

"That couple that was pulled out of the lake. The boy, Steffen, told us they were both wearing clothes. Ordinary clothes. He said he thought it was odd that they weren't even wearing jackets. And another thing he noticed was that the woman was wearing a suit and tie, whereas the man was wearing a red dress. That struck me as odd, but I left it out of the article, since it didn't seem important."

Jens-Ole was quiet for a little while, then he cleared his throat. "Sounds like something you should look into. They might have been drunk and fallen into the water, but ask around. If your nose tells you something's off, then I trust that cute little nose of yours."

"Thanks, Jens-Ole," I said, chuckling. I gave Sara a thumbs-up and she smiled back.

"Don't let me down," Jens-Ole yelled from the other end.

"I won't."

"I owe you one," I said to Sara when I had hung up.

She laughed. "My pleasure."

"Have they mentioned anything on the scanner about the bodies today?"

"They haven't, and that struck me as a little odd as well. Yesterday, they talked about it constantly. But today, there's nothing. They're all very quiet. It's very unusual for them."

"Hm." I walked to the kitchen and grabbed another cup of coffee. Sara had bought pastry, and it was sitting in a bag. I grabbed a couple and put them on a plate, then served one for Sara. We ate and drank coffee in silence in front of our computers for a little while.

"Is Sune coming in today?" Sara suddenly asked.

I shrugged. "I know he had an assignment for some magazine early this morning, but that shouldn't take long. Other than that, he's not doing anything. I don't have anything for him yet."

"Maybe you should call him and ask him to come in," she said, sounding very secretive. "Let him use his computer skills a little bit."

I nodded with a smile. I knew exactly what she meant.

"I'll text him right away."

10

Lise Knudsen was upset. She grabbed her bike and rode it along the Fjord with tears rolling across her cheeks. In the distance, she could see the white church peeking up between the old houses. For all of her seventy-six years, she had lived in Karrebaeksminde; she had gone to this church every Sunday. She had gone there with her parents as a child, and again as an adult with her husband and two children. She had loved going there, and thought it was the right thing to do, the right way to bring up her children.

"Direct your children onto the right path, and when they are older, they will not leave it," she would always say, quoting the Bible, when her husband protested that they had to go every Sunday when he would rather stay at home and sleep in.

Despite her husband's many protests, Lise Knudsen had always been an eager churchgoer and rarely missed a sermon. And, she had liked Pastor Kemp when she became pastor of Karrebaeksminde Church some fifty years ago. Lise had enjoyed her sermons and thought of her as having a fresh perspective. She was frank and always said things the way she saw them. Lise had liked her directness.

But she felt the dear pastor had gone too far this past weekend. She had told the congregation that all homosexuals were sinners and would rot in hell. It had upset Lise in a way she had never suspected.

After her husband, Finn, had suffered a stroke last month and passed away, Lise had discovered something about him that he had kept a deep secret from her for all of their years of marriage. In his closet, behind all his clothes, she found a suitcase. To her chagrin, it was filled with women's clothing... dresses, skirts, stockings, and high heels. Lise hadn't understood what it all was until she called her daughter, who had explained it to her.

"Dad was a transsexual, Mom. I thought you knew?"

Lise had almost suffered a stroke herself. "He was what?"

"He dressed up in women's clothes when you weren't home, or when he was on business trips. You mean to tell me you never knew this, Mom? Per and I have known since we were teenagers. We walked in on him one day when school was let out earlier than usual and he was home alone. He was dancing with the vacuum cleaner in the living room, wearing a gorgeous purple dress and stilettos. We always assumed you knew about it, but chose to never talk about it."

"I...I...I never did."

Ever since the conversation with her daughter, Lise had wondered about the husband she thought she knew. She couldn't say she understood him or what he had been, but she knew that she still loved him. If he was gay, she never knew, but she should have suspected it, since he hadn't seemed interested in her sexually since they'd had the children. She always assumed he'd simply lost interest in her, and since she was raised to believe that sex and lust were sinful, she had never enjoyed the act, and realized she liked not having to do it anymore.

She never thought it could be because of *that*.

In the weeks after the discovery, Lise Knudsen realized it didn't change the way she felt about her late husband, to discover that what saddened her was the fact that he had led a double life that she hadn't known about, that he didn't feel comfortable enough with her to talk about it. That's what troubled her the most. Until last Sunday, when Pastor Kemp, with thunder, declared that all gay and transgender people would go to hell.

"It's a sin, no matter what you call it," she had yelled from the pulpit.

It wasn't the first time Pastor Kemp had declared something like that, but it was the first time Lise Knudsen had listened thoroughly, and now she was upset. She hadn't been able to stop wondering if Henning was going to burn for eternity, just because he liked to dress as a woman. Just because he might have been gay? It didn't seem fair. Henning had been such a loving father. Such a good husband. Was he supposed to suffer for eternity because of this strange double life? It wasn't right. Not in Lise Knudsen's book. There had to be some sort of redemption for people who otherwise led decent lives and were good to others, right? Henning hadn't been a bad person; he had been the best among people…always caring, always loving. It couldn't be right that he should be punished like this. It simply couldn't. Where was the love in that?

Lise had thought about this for a long time, and now she was going to talk to the pastor about it. She would ask her if there was some chance that Henning could have been forgiven. Wasn't it so that the Lord had taken all of our sins when He died on the cross? Couldn't He have taken Henning's then?

Lise sniffled and parked the bike by the red wooden fence at the entrance to the church. She locked it and started walking across the gravel. She grabbed the handle to the heavy wooden door and pushed it open.

"Pastor Kemp?" she said, as she walked in.

Candles were lit at the altar, and it looked like someone was in there.

"Pastor Kemp?" Lise Knudsen said again, as she walked closer to the figure. "I have a question about Heaven and Hell that I need to get clarified."

She blinked her eyes. It was hard to see what it was…if it was a person or something else.

Damn these old eyes.

She walked a few steps closer, then she stopped with a gasp. Lise Knudsen held a hand to her chest and gasped for air. In front of her, attached to the old wooden cross, stared the pastor back at her with open lifeless eyes.

11

"Sorry I'm late. I ran into our new neighbor."

Sune threw his jacket on the chair before he sprang for coffee. It was past lunchtime, and I had been waiting for him for several hours. I followed him into the kitchen. "What do you mean new neighbor?"

Sune sipped his coffee. The tip of his nose and ears were red from the cold. "Well, it's technically your dad's neighbor, but we live there too, at least until we find something else, right?"

I sighed and grabbed some coffee as well. It had been a discussion subject for what felt like forever now. Sune was tired of living in my dad's house with him and wanted us to buy our own place, whereas I thought it was practical to be close to my dad so I could better take care of him. I understood why Sune was tired of it, but I wasn't sure I was ready to move out yet. I felt bad for my dad. He loved having us there.

"So, what was he like?" I asked, blowing on my cup.

"Seemed like a nice guy," Sune said. "We just talked for a few minutes, that's all. He's renting the house."

"Any kids?"

"No."

"Wife?"

"Just went through a bad breakup."

"Ah."

"Yeah, well…" Sune sipped his coffee. "You got work for me?"

"Yes. I want you to get me into the autopsy report on the couple that was found in the lake on Sunday. Could you do that?"

Sune shrugged and sipped his coffee again. "Are you asking if I can or if I will?"

I made a grimace. "Just do it, alright?"

Sune laughed. "I will. But why? I thought it was just a drowning accident?"

"That's what they've been telling the press, but I have a feeling it was something else. It was something the boy said during the interview. They weren't exactly dressed to be fishing. And only hardcore fishermen would go out in this cold, and they would definitely dress for it."

Sune nodded pensively while drinking more coffee. He grabbed a pastry from the bag and put it in his mouth.

"Besides, the boy said the woman was dressed in a suit and tie, while the man was in a dress. I want to know if that's right. I also want to know how they died. I tried to call the forensics department, but they said they couldn't tell me since it's an ongoing investigation."

"So, they think it's murder?" Sune asked.

"I asked them the very same question, but they said they couldn't answer that," I said, and started walking back towards my desk.

"To be fair then, a drowning accident needs to be investigated as well," he said. "They can't tell you anything until they have all the facts."

"I know, but I'm just not buying it," I said, and pointed at the newspaper's computer. I never used it, since I had my laptop, but it was perfect for Sune. If anyone tracked him, they would never know it was actually him. The newspaper would have to take the fall, which they were prepared to do. I had made that deal with Jens-Ole. It would never fall back on Sune, no matter what.

Sune turned it on and pulled up a chair. I returned to my own screen and let him do his magic. I looked at Sara, who suddenly seemed preoccupied with what was happening on the police scanner. Her eyes met mine, and I understood it was serious.

12

"Something is going on at the church," Sara finally said. She looked at me intensely. I could tell she was agitated. Her cheeks were blushing.

"Like what?" I asked.

"I don't know, but they've called all cars to go there…code fourteen." Sara took off her headset and stared at me. "Possible homicide."

I turned and looked at Sune. "We should go," I said.

He got up and grabbed his camera.

I put my jacket on, and then rushed down the stairs with Sune right after me. We drove across town and ran a couple of red lights. I figured all the police cars were occupied, so no one would notice. There was hardly any traffic, so it took only a few minutes to reach the church. Three police cars were parked in front. A fourth arrived when we did.

"Sara was right," I said, and parked the car. "This is big."

We jumped out of the car. Sune was shooting pictures as we walked towards the entrance. His finger was constantly working the camera, shooting everything.

"They haven't blocked the entrance with tape yet," I whispered, as we came closer.

We walked with determined steps past the police cars and onto the gravel. Sune was still shooting. The church door was open as we walked up, and someone walked inside. I grabbed the door before it closed, and pulled it open again. Sune shot pictures like crazy, while I held my breath.

The sight that met us was excruciating. It was really bad. A woman, dressed in a suit and tie and a top hat, was attached to a wooden cross with nails through her hands. She had been crucified. Two officers were working on getting the cross down.

"Hey! What are you doing here?" A voice yelled from inside the church. An officer had spotted us, and came running towards us. The sound of his voice echoed in the old church building.

"Let's go," I said, and closed the door.

We walked away as the officer came up behind us. "You two. Stop."

We stopped and turned to look at him. He was fairly handsome, tall with blond hair and blue eyes.

"What are you doing here?" he asked, pointing his baton at me. "You're not supposed to be here."

I showed him my press card. *"Zeeland Times.* We heard something was going on and wanted to see what it was, Officer…?"

"Pedersen. Henrik Pedersen. And you're Rebekka Franck, huh? I read all your articles. We went to the same high school. We lived down the street from you in number fourteen. I was one grade under you, but you probably don't remember me."

"Pedersen. Oh, yeah. Now I do. You had a sister, right?"

"Yes."

"I remember her. I used to play with her."

"Yes, that's right."

"So, what happened here?" I asked, hoping to exploit the fact that I knew the guy a little, even if I didn't remember him, only remembered his sister. Henrik Pedersen looked around before he leaned over and spoke quietly.

"I'm sorry. I really can't say anything. You know how it is. This is a police investigation."

Just as he spoke, two vans from the forensic department in Copenhagen drove up. I looked at them, then back at the officer. "I think it's fair to say that you can't hide the facts anymore, Officer. We're talking murder here, right?"

He looked like he really wanted to help me. "You know I can't say much yet. Not until the crime scene technicians have done their job. But, between you and me, yes. It's definitely murder."

"I won't quote you on that, Officer," I said with a smile. "Who was it? Who was on the cross?"

The officer looked around to see if anyone was listening, then he whispered. "The pastor. It was the pastor. Someone nailed the woman to the cross like freaking Jesus."

"What about the clothes?" I asked. "It didn't look much like the pastor's usual robe, did it?"

"I can't comment on that."

"I won't quote you on it. I saw it with my own eyes, remember?" I said.

Officer Pedersen leaned over and whispered. "It was a suit and hat. Strange, huh?"

As he spoke, another officer approached us. He looked angry. "Officer Pedersen? You're needed inside," he said.

"Yes, sir." Officer Pedersen looked away. He stormed inside.

I recognized the officer as Chief Superintendent Bergman, newly appointed head of the Karrebaeksminde police department. I'd had meetings with the superintendent several times before. Usually, he was polite and ready to talk, but not today. He looked at us with fury in his eyes.

"You two better get out of here," he said. "We don't want any press on this case."

"Can you confirm it is a homicide?" I asked.

"I told you, we don't want any press on this case."

"Is it related to the bodies found in the lake?" I asked.

Superintendent Bergman stared at me. His eyes went almost black.

"GET OUT OF HERE!"

13

"That was strange."

Sune looked at me when we got back to the car.

"I mean, how he reacted. He looked like he wanted to grab us and throw us out of there."

I unlocked the car. "It *was* weird," I said. "Usually, he's a very gentle guy, very friendly and someone I can talk to."

We got in and I started the car. "Could it be my question?" I asked. "Did I strike a nerve or something?"

"It sure looked like it. I mean, he was angry at first, but he didn't get really mean until you asked him if the two cases were related."

I drove off, while trying to shake off the experience of the superintendent yelling at me like that. It was quite uncomfortable.

"They must be, but why did that make him so mad at me?" I said, as we were back on the main road leading through town.

"Maybe he's nervous?" Sune suggested. "Maybe the case is troubling him or something? Maybe he just had a bad day."

"You can say that again," I said, and parked in front of the newspaper's offices downtown. I got out and went into the small building. Sara was still listening to the scanner as we entered.

"Anything new?" I asked.

"Nope. Except they have told everyone to avoid any contact with the press whatsoever. No one is allowed to talk to journalists."

"That's odd," I said, and sat down by my computer. Sune returned to his in the corner. "I mean, they're usually happy to talk to us, and use us to help in search of suspects and so on. They might keep secrets from us, but they don't usually keep us completely out like this."

"Maybe they're afraid of spreading panic," Sara said. "You know how easily people get scared."

"True, but still…" I paused and drank a sip of water from my bottle. There was something going on here that I didn't like. Why would they try and keep the press completely out of this? If anything, they needed us to search for eyewitnesses and so on. We always helped each other. I didn't understand.

"I think I know why," Sune suddenly said.

I looked at him across the room.

"I got the autopsy. You were right; the man was wearing a dress and the woman a suit and tie…"

"Just like the pastor," I interrupted him. "Someone's trying to make a statement here. A spectacular one indeed. The bodies are on display. He wants us to find the bodies. He wants us to hear his message."

"And, he's a police officer."

I almost choked. "What was that?"

Sune shrugged. "The two victims in the lake were both beaten to death with a baton. The same type the officers use. It says so right here. They know exactly what kind of bruises a baton creates, and on the couple there were even black marks left from the rubber. The Danish police batons are made from metal, but covered in black rubber. They tested the rubber found on the skin of the bodies, and it is the same type used for making the police batons in this country."

I leaned back in my chair. "Well, I'll be damned..."

"Isn't it possible for normal people to buy a baton like that online or something?" Sara asked.

I nodded pensively. "It might be, but we need to look into that. There are several possibilities; it could be stolen or something, but it could also be an officer. It would certainly explain why the police are trying to keep the press out of this, why they are reacting so aggressively towards us. I can hardly write any of this in the paper, but at least it gives us something to work with."

"There's more," Sune said.

"What?" I asked.

"The bodies have been mutilated."

"What do you mean mutilated?" I asked, fearing slightly for the answer.

He looked up from his screen and his eyes met mine.

"Their genitals have been cut off."

14

"I WANT TO SHAVE TOO. I want to shave myself!" Alex yelled.

It was one of his first childhood memories. At least one of the strongest. At age five, he had watched his dad shave, then asked if he could shave too. His father had given him an empty razor and some shaving cream to play with. Then, Alex came into the bathroom.

"I want to shave too," she said.

Their father stared at her. "Girls don't shave," he said. "Go find your mom. She can help you put on some make-up or nail polish instead."

"I don't want make-up," Alex said, tears forming in her eyes. "I want to shave. I want to shave! Why can't I shave?"

"Sweetie. You're a girl. Girls don't grow beards," their father said, almost aggressively.

"I don't think I'm a girl. I don't feel like a girl. I don't want to be a girl. What is wrong with me?"

The man remembered the nightly questions from his sister while he sat in the chair of his living room. The questions haunted him.

"What if they're all wrong and I'm really a boy?" she would ask when she climbed into his bed at night.

"I don't know, Alex."

She wanted them to call her Alex. Her real name was Alexandra, but she didn't like to be called that. Just like she didn't like to wear all those dresses that their mom would force her to, even on freezing winter days.

"Small girls wear dresses," she would say, when Alex screamed and tried to rip her dress off in one of her many tantrums that became more and more frequent the older they got. By the time they reached the age of ten, she required all of their parents' attention, and the boy slid more and more into the background. It was all about Alex. They took her to see doctors and therapists. She was out of control, they told her parents.

"I hate all of them. I don't want to be a girl," she would tell him at night, crying. He would comfort her, feeling the pain she felt inside. On nights when their father had whipped her for dressing in jeans or cutting her hair, the boy would hold her in his arms while she cried, even though he himself felt the pain on his back almost as bad as she did.

It was on those nights that he started cursing his parents, the pastor, and all the doctors for what they were trying to do to his sister. Why couldn't they just let her be who she was? Was it so wrong? Was it such a bad thing?

"I'm not a girl. I'm not a girl!" she would scream at them again and again. The man could still hear her voice in his mind, over and over again. He had tried for years to escape it, but it wouldn't go away. The pain was still there. He still felt it. He had hoped killing the pastor and making her pay for what she had done would silence the voices in his head and ease the pain a little. But it hadn't. On the contrary. He almost felt like the pain had become deeper and the voices stronger.

It's all your fault. You know it, don't you? You did this to her.

You didn't stop them. You knew she was in pain. You knew how bad it was. You felt her pain. And yet you never did anything. You never even spoke up, you coward.

The man felt tears roll across his cheeks. How he loathed these long lonely evenings. How he hated being without Alex.

15

"By the way, I invited our new neighbor for dinner tonight."

Sune looked at me and shrugged. "Sorry to spring that on you this late. I completely forgot."

I had already started dinner, and was standing in the kitchen putting the layers in the lasagna. "You're kidding me, right?"

"Sorry," he said. "I completely forgot. He seemed like he needed the company. I felt a little bad for him. His girlfriend recently left him, and he's all alone. He just moved here. He doesn't know anyone around the neighborhood."

"Couldn't you have said so a little earlier? I'm not sure there's enough food now. I would have made more," I said, annoyed.

"Sorry. I forgot."

I grumbled, then opened the cabinet to see if there was anything I could warm as a supplement to my lasagna and salad. I didn't find anything and opened the freezer. I found a bag of frozen carrots. "Guess that will have to do," I said, and defrosted them.

THIRTEEN, FOURTEEN... LITTLE BOY UNSEEN

The doorbell rang. I felt tired and not in the mood to meet new people.

"That's probably him," Sune said, and sprang for the door.

I found my most enchanting smile.

"Hi there," Sune said, and they exchanged a fist bump. As the guy stepped into the light of the hallway, I realized why Sune had been so eager to invite this guy over. He was in his late twenties, about the same age as Sune. It made sense. Sune was always hanging out with my friends and me. We were all in our thirties, and of course he needed someone a little younger to talk to every now and then. The two of them seemed to hit it off extremely well.

"This is Rebekka," Sune said. "Rebekka meet Jeppe."

The guy stepped forward with a shy smile. "Hello," he said. I shook his hand. He seemed like he would rather have given me a fist bump as well.

Sune grabbed his shoulder. "Come meet the kids."

Sune pulled Jeppe into the living room, where the kids were playing on the X-box. I returned to the kitchen, where William was sitting in his playpen, trying to fit square blocks into round holes. I chopped the salad, and put in tomatoes and some broccoli to make it fill more.

"So, who's the new guy?" My dad entered the kitchen, leaning on his cane.

I smiled. He hadn't been out of bed all day. He was very pale. He had lost a lot of weight from lying still. He suddenly looked so old. I kissed his cheek and helped him sit on one of the kitchen chairs.

"That's Jeppe. He just moved in next door."

"That's good," my dad said. "Sune got a friend to play with."

I chuckled. That was exactly how I felt. Just like when you go somewhere and your kid finds someone to play with. I felt a little relieved. Maybe Sune would stop nagging me about moving out and getting our own place.

"You talk to your sister lately?" my dad asked.

"Not since Christmas. Why?"

I felt a pinch of guilt. My sister lived fifteen minutes from us, yet I didn't see her much. She was always busy with her career and family, and she always made sure I knew how great she was doing. I didn't like to spend much time with her, since I hated how she always criticized me and rubbed in my face how perfect she was. Plus, she had cared for my dad in the years after our mother died, so when I returned to Karrebaeksminde, she saw it as her way to get out of having to care for him anymore. It was my turn.

"Maybe I should call her," I said. "Maybe tomorrow."

"Do that. Now, is dinner ready soon?"

"As a matter of fact, it is," I said, and looked at the timer on the stove. It rang at that exact moment, and I pulled out the lasagna.

"Dinner!" I yelled.

I placed the lasagna on the table and waited for the sound of feet running towards the kitchen, but it remained quiet.

"Maybe they didn't hear you," my dad said.

"Maybe." I walked to the living room, where they were all sitting in front of the TV, while Jeppe was holding the controller for the X-box.

"He's really good at playing Skylander, Mom," Julie said.

Tobias looked at Jeppe with sparkling eyes. "Good? He's excellent!" he exclaimed.

Sune seemed to be the most excited of them all. "You should have seen what he just did."

"And he knows all the cheat codes, Mom," Julie said.

"That's all very nice, dear, but dinner is on the table."

"Ah, Mom," Julie said. "We were having so much fun."

"Yeah," Tobias agreed.

"Can't we eat in here?" Jeppe asked.

I stared, baffled, at the man my boyfriend had invited. He looked like a kid with the controller between his hands.

"Yeah!" Tobias said.

"Yeah, let's do that, Mom," Julie said.

I stared at the two of them and shook my head. "No way."

It was nice to see them agree on something, though, and not fight about everything like they had been doing lately. But I wasn't going to have dinner in the living room and have lasagna all over the couch and carpet.

"Oh, come on, Mom," Julie said

"Yes, come on, Mom," Sune repeated. "Jeppe is about to show us something epic."

"Please?" Julie said.

I stared at the pack, who were now all watching me with pleading eyes. What was this? Were they all ganging up on me now? I couldn't believe them. Especially not Sune.

"Please," Sune said.

"You're kidding me, right?" I said. I felt like I had a room full of kids. Even Jeppe was making pleading eyes at me.

"No!" I said. "I have made dinner, and I want us to eat it at the table together as a family."

"Aw," they said in unison. They all looked sad as they got up from the floor.

I hated being the one to ruin all the fun and felt anger build up towards Sune for not backing me up in this. He walked past me and put his arm on Jeppe's shoulder. They looked like they had known each other all of their lives.

"You'll just have to show us afterwards, right?" Sune said.

"Sure," Jeppe said.

"Yay," the kids cheered, as they walked into the kitchen where my dad was waiting.

16

THEY LITERALLY SHOVELED DINNER DOWN. Never had I seen my kids eat this fast. Or Sune, for that matter. None of them seemed to take any notice of the food or me. Sune was busy talking to Jeppe about games and computer hacking, which apparently, they also had in common.

I was divided about this situation. I was happy for Sune, that he had made a new friend, but I wasn't sure I liked the way he simply ignored me.

"So, Jeppe, where are you from originally?" I asked, trying to make some adult conversation that didn't have to do with computers.

Jeppe looked at me, and was about to answer, when Sune threw his fork on his plate. "I'm done. Anyone want to go back and see what else Jeppe can do?"

"Yaaay!" the kids yelled.

William squeezed a lump of lasagna between his fingers, and I had to wipe it off and give him his fork. Tobias and Julie got up and followed Sune and Jeppe into the living room without taking their plates out as they usually did.

I looked at my dad. "Can you believe them?"

My dad chuckled, then patted me on my shoulder. "Don't make a big deal about it," he said. "They're just having fun."

"I know." I sighed and ate another piece of lasagna. "But I'm not a part of it. I feel like the kid that is being left out in school."

"Then go join them," he said.

I patted his hand on the table and shook my head. "Nah. I'd rather spend time with you. I don't know anything about their games, and I don't want to. Maybe I should just let it go, huh? Let them have their thing."

"That's my girl," my dad said, and drank his cranberry juice that I bought for him. It was supposed prevent another bladder infection. The doctor had told me it would help. His last infection nearly killed him.

I finished my portion and helped my dad back upstairs. He smiled wearily when I kissed him and turned out the light. I had a bad feeling inside when I left the room, and wondered how long I would still have him. I didn't dare to think of the day when he wasn't here anymore. I was going to miss him so terribly. That was probably why I wasn't in a hurry to find our own place yet. I wanted to spend as much time with him as possible, before it was too late.

I put William to bed, sang a couple of songs for him, then left his room and walked downstairs. I started cleaning up after our dinner, just as my phone rang. Unknown number. I picked it up.

"Hello?"

"Hi, Rebekka. This is David. Is this a bad time?"

I looked in the direction of the living room, where the kids were screaming in excitement. Sune was being the loudest of all of them.

"No. Not at all. Actually, I'm kind of glad to hear from you," I said, and sat on a kitchen chair.

"Oh, good. I don't want to cause you any trouble. I sensed I wasn't exactly welcome the last time I was at your house, and wondered if everything is okay?"

"Everything's fine, I guess."

"Ah, but see, there's the problem. I can tell it's not fine. I can hear it in your voice."

"It's a long story," I said with a sigh. I suddenly longed for a cigarette. I hadn't smoked in a long time, not since I got pregnant with William. I hadn't thought much about it, but now I did. I felt like the walls of the house were closing in on me and I couldn't breathe. I needed to get out before I started screaming.

"Listen. Do you want to meet up?" I asked. "I was thinking about going for a walk. Get out of the house a little. Maybe you would like to join me?"

17

I told Sune I was going out for a walk, which wasn't a lie, then told him William was sleeping upstairs. He was so occupied with the game and Jeppe, I wasn't sure he even heard me. Julie did, however, and she said she would listen for William waking up.

I kissed her on the forehead. I knew she would be responsible and make sure Sune took care of William, just in case.

"I'll only be gone for a little while," I said, and left.

I met David at the marina, where I bought a package of cigarettes and two beers at a small newsstand. We sat on a bench. The marina seemed so desolate in the winter. In the summer, it was always buzzing with people from all the big yachts and sailboats.

An old fishing boat was swaying in the water in front of us. We chatted a little about this and that, and then shared a few memories from our time inside the limestone mines.

"So, what brought you to Karrebaeksminde?" I asked, and handed him a cigarette.

"Can I be completely honest?" he asked.

"Of course," I said, and pulled out a cigarette and put it in my mouth. He lit it for me and lit his own. It tasted so good. I felt guilty afterwards, but continued anyway. I felt like I deserved it somehow.

David looked at me. "I came because of you."

I coughed and drank some beer to make it stop. "I'm sorry, what?"

"I came to see you. Ever since I left that hospital, I haven't been able to stop thinking about you."

Uh-oh! I had not seen that coming. How had I not seen this? I was just happy to see him.

"David, I'm…I have a boyfriend; we have a child together…"

"I know. I know. That's not why I'm here. I just…I just feel like talking to you. You're the only person who truly understands me. Who knows what I've been through and who…you know…gets it."

I nodded. I had to admit I felt the same way. It was so hard to explain to people what I had been through that I had simply stopped trying. I just kept it all bottled up inside of me, and it made me miserable. I knew it did.

"I know what you mean," I said, even though I feared I might be leading him on. I wasn't looking for anything romantic, I hoped he understood that, but I had hoped he could be my friend. I needed one. I needed an adult to talk to, one that understood me. And he did.

"I've tried psychologists," David said. "I've tried therapists; my doctor even suggested medicine to help me sleep, but I didn't want it. Nothing has worked so far. I feel so wrong, no matter where I am. Except when I'm with you. Is that weird?"

"A little," I said with a light chuckle. "But I feel the same. Most days I'm simply surviving. You know, making it through, even though I feel like I'm constantly in the wrong place. Like I've changed somehow. It's hard to explain. It's like I want more now. I can't just get by anymore. I want the most out of every moment of my life now. I don't want to miss a second of my kids' lives; I don't want to miss the last of my dad's. I feel like I'm drifting in this sea of indifference, like I'm on a hamster wheel that I can't escape. I feel like everyone is on it, but not everyone knows. Like I have somehow had my eyes opened to it, like it has been revealed to me, and now I don't want to waste my life running inside of it anymore." I paused and looked at him.

He stared at me.

"You think I'm nuts, don't you?" I said.

"No, not at all. That's exactly how I feel. I was in this black hole when the accident happened. I've never told anyone this, but I was actually about to kill myself when the ground opened up underneath my brother's house. I was that depressed. Being swallowed into the sinkhole was probably the best thing that could have happened to me at that point. I have started to see it as a blessing, like a divine intervention of some sort. I usually don't believe in that sort of thing, but…I don't know. It's just…It has changed everything."

I smoked my cigarette and looked at the fishing boat. It was such a relief to finally talk to someone whom I could be completely honest with. Someone who didn't think I was crazy for thinking and feeling the way I did.

"My only problem is, I don't know what to do with it," I said. "I don't know how to break out of the hamster wheel, how to escape the indifference, how to live a life that really matters."

David smoked his cigarette as well. "Me either," he said. "I hoped you could help me figure it out. That's the real reason why I came here. I thought you, somehow, were the answer."

18

"Good morning!"

Jeppe peeked his head over the hedge with a smile. He scared the crap out of me, and I couldn't stop the feeling that he'd been waiting behind the hedge for me to walk to my car.

"Have a nice day at work," he said with a cheerful voice, and then added, "Tonight, I'll bring some chicken wings for dinner."

I was completely taken aback. Jeppe smiled a little shyly, and I couldn't help feeling sorry for him. He was all alone in that house. But I also really wanted my family back. I didn't want him to come over for dinner again. Still, I couldn't really say anything but, "Okay."

I drove off, feeling strange. Sune was going to drop off the kids, as usual, since he never had anything to do until nine at the earliest. Today, he didn't have anything yet. As a freelance photographer, he would sometimes wait at home for hours until they suddenly called him to go somewhere. Sometimes, they would book him a few days in advance, but that was rare. As a matter of fact, he hadn't had as much to do as he used to, and it was getting to him a little. There were

THIRTEEN, FOURTEEN... LITTLE BOY UNSEEN

entire days when he didn't have any work to do, and he hated that.

I hoped we would get something at the paper today. We had come far on the story about the killings, but I still couldn't get anything confirmed by the police, so I couldn't write it. Jens-Ole thought about making one of those, *The Newspaper learns from a reliable source that...*articles, but up until now, I had refused that. I hated those kinds of stories, where you knew a lot of stuff, but couldn't document it. So, I let the story linger for a little while, and instead decided to do a story about a couple that were building an organic house made entirely of sand on Enoe, the island outside of Karrebaeksminde. It was one of those stories with great pictures and it would be easy to write. I needed that. Jens-Ole liked the idea, and I called Sune to get him to be the photographer on it. He didn't answer his phone.

"That's odd," I said to Sara. "He always answers his phone. He has to if he wants to work."

I got a worried feeling in my stomach, wondering if there was something wrong, maybe something happened to one of the kids? I called him again, but still nothing.

"I'm gonna go home and pick him up," I said to Sara, then grabbed my stuff and walked to my car. I drove home and rushed inside.

"Sune?"

No answer. The living room was empty, so was the kitchen. I ran upstairs, calling his name again.

"Sune?"

I opened the door to my dad's bedroom. He was sound asleep, so I closed it again before I checked the kids' bedrooms.

Maybe he went grocery shopping? Yes, that's it. He went to shop and couldn't hear his phone. That has to be it.

I left the house and drove downtown to his favorite shopping center. I walked towards SuperBrugsen, where we always shopped, when I passed the Internet Café next to it, and spotted Sune's bike parked outside.

"You've got to be kidding me?" I said.

I opened the door and walked into the darkness, only lit by the many screens. Loads of teenagers skipping school were staring at them, playing games where they were holding big guns.

"What the...?" I spotted Sune by one of the computers, and next to him sat Jeppe by another computer screen wearing a headset. They were grinning and poking each other, eating chips, and drinking sodas.

"What's going on here?" I asked, and pulled Sune's headset off.

"Oh, hi, Rebekka. What are you doing here?" Sune said.

"I have a job for you. Are you not picking up your phone anymore?"

Sune grabbed his phone from the table. "Sorry. I didn't hear it," he said.

"I'm sorry, Rebekka," Jeppe said. "I thought I'd take him out and have a little fun. He seemed so bored at the house."

I forced a smile. "Well, Sune can't play anymore."

19

EXACTLY WHEN THEIR parents consulted the doctor for help, the man couldn't remember, but he remembered going to the clinic numerous times during his childhood. He remembered driving for a long time, then sitting in a strange office furnished with a couch, Oriental rugs, and lots of plants that reminded him more of a living room than a doctor's office. He also remembered the pictures and sculptures of erect phalluses and vaginas. But, most of all, he remembered how his sister hated the doctor. How she loathed coming to his office. How she would scream and yell every time they told her that's where they were going.

Their parents, on the other hand, adored the doctor. The man remembered how his mother listened attentively to everything the doctor said, and how his words soon became law in their home.

As just a young boy, the man hadn't always understand what the doctor had talked about when they visited his office, but he did remember one thing the doctor always told them. He believed *that gender identity developed primarily as a result of social learning from early childhood, and that it could be changed with the appropriate behavioral interventions.*

"What's behavioral interventions?" the boy asked his mother one day, shortly after their first visit to the doctor's office, when they were alone in the kitchen.

"Don't you worry about that," his mother answered, and kissed his forehead. "But I can tell it's what's gonna help your sister. I tell you, this doctor is going to change everything for us. Your sister is in the best possible hands. Things are finally looking bright for us."

The boy would soon enough learn exactly what *behavioral intervention* was. The doctor worked with a therapist, who had hair as white as snow and eyes so blue they looked purple. The therapist came to the house one day and watched the twins as they played in the yard. He observed them for hours, while their mother looked with anxious eyes from behind the window in the kitchen. Then, he grumbled and wrote on his notepad.

The next time the therapist arrived, he spoke for a long time with their parents before he came into the yard and called the twins to approach him.

"Let's play a new game, shall we? I have one for you. I would like for you, Alexandra, to lie down on the grass now on all fours, then I would like for your brother to get behind your sister's butt with your crotch against your sister's buttocks. I want you both to do thrusting movements. Now, try that."

Thinking it was just a game, they obeyed the therapist, while he watched them and made notes in his black book.

"Now, I want you, Alexandra…"

"I'm Alex," his sister replied defiantly.

"No. You're Alexandra. That is your real name. Now, I want you to lie down on your back with your legs spread, with your brother on top, and again do the thrusting movements. Now, go."

The exercises went on and on, once a week for years, and the therapist became a regular part of the twin's lives, not one they enjoyed much, especially not when they were one day told to take off their clothes and engage in *genital inspections*, while he took pictures. When their parents protested, the therapist simply stated that it was an important part of the treatment, since *childhood was sexual rehearsal play* and that laid the foundation for a *healthy adult gender identity*.

After that, no one questioned the therapist's methods, since it was all in the best interest of Alex, but the boy saw how it affected his sister, how a sadness started to grow inside of her. She knew how much trouble she was to her family, how much they wanted to change her, and that sowed a seed of self-loathing that soon started eating her from the inside. Not only would she cry at night, she also started hurting herself with whatever she could get her hands on. Once, he found her cutting herself with scissors. She was sitting in her bed at night, just letting the blood run from her wrists onto the bed, soaking the sheet. Terrified, he pulled the scissors away, then grabbed her in his arms and held her tight.

"Don't EVER do that again!"

Alex tried to pull away while crying, "I'm an alien. I am an ALIEN!"

"No, you're not. You're my sister. You hear me? I can't live without you!"

"How can I be your sister? I'm not a girl; I'm not a boy. If I'm not an alien, then who am I?"

The boy had no answer for that.

20

"I can't believe you."

We were driving across the bridge leading to Enoe when I had finally calmed down enough to talk. Sune sat with his camera between his hands. He didn't look at me.

"I just wanted to have a little fun," he grumbled. "Jeppe came over and asked if I wanted to go. Geez. Calm down, would you?"

I took in a deep breath and remembered my dad's advice.

Don't make a big deal of it, I told myself. *It's not like he did anything really bad. It's not like he cheated on you.*

But it felt like it. I guess that was why I reacted like I did. I felt like he was slipping away, like someone was pulling him out of my hands. Someone younger and more fun.

"I'm sorry," I said. "I just didn't want you to miss out on this assignment. And I hate when you don't answer your phone. Ever since the accident, I've been so scared of something happening to you or the kids. I guess it's just what happens when you realize how fast your life can change, how fragile your life is…"

I paused and thought about David. We had talked about

this yesterday at the port. I was suddenly overwhelmed with guilt. I hadn't told Sune I had been with David. It was wrong.

"Sune…I…"

I didn't get any further before Sune interrupted me. "Sometimes you act like you think you're my mother. I really don't like that. It's got to stop, Rebekka. I'm a grown man. I'm allowed to do what I want to."

"You're right," I said, as we reached Enoe and drove towards the beach. It was one of those gray January days where the sun simply didn't bother to peek out through the thick layer of clouds. It would set in the early afternoon anyway, so I couldn't really blame it.

"I'll get better at this, okay?"

"Jeppe even says that you…"

"Wait a minute…Jeppe?" I said. "Is that where all of this is suddenly coming from?"

"No. I've been thinking about it for a while. Jeppe just said yesterday that he thought it seemed like you were my mother."

"Well, stop acting like a child, then," I said.

I stopped the car in front of a lot. The foundation for the house was almost in, and five workers were working on finishing it. I spotted a couple that I believed had to be the future owners of the country's first sand house.

"Excuse me?" Sune said. "Who is it that takes care of the kids every morning and makes sure they get to school? Who picks them up when you're too busy? Who does all the housework at home? Who grocery shops? Who vacuums and cleans and washes all the clothes?"

I exhaled and forced a smile as the couple approached us. I had spoken to them over the phone and arranged for them to meet us there for the interview.

"I know, baby. I know you do most of the work, especially

lately, since you haven't had so many assignments. I know you do. And I appreciate it. I truly do. I'm sorry."

I looked at him. Our eyes locked.

"Okay then," he said and smiled. "All I'm asking is to be allowed to have some fun now and then."

"Got it."

"Now, let's shoot this baby, so I can get back to Jeppe."

Sune jumped out of the car while I looked at him.

Get back to Jeppe?

I couldn't help feeling that pinch of jealousy again. The guy had been in our lives for two days now, and already Sune was more excited about hanging out with him than me. I mean, of course he was allowed to have friends. I could hardly be angry about that.

I shook the feeling and exited the car. The couple building the sand house approached me and we shook hands.

"Rebekka Franck, *Zeeland Times*. This is my photographer, Sune. If you don't mind, he'll be shooting pictures while we speak. So, you're building a house of sand? How on earth did you come up with that idea?"

21

"Your one o'clock is here, Doctor"

"Let him in," the voice sounded from the intercom.

"You can go in now. It's through that door," the secretary said.

The man rose to his feet and walked to the door. He paused as he laid his hand on the handle and pulled it down.

"Welcome," the therapist's voice said as he entered.

They shook hands.

"I'm Dr. Korner. Please sit down."

The man did as he was told and sat on the couch. He put his backpack on the floor.

"So, have you ever seen a therapist before?" Dr. Korner asked.

The man repressed a smile. "You could say that."

"And what does that mean?"

"I saw one…in my childhood."

Dr. Korner noted that in his notepad. "I see. So, you're familiar with how this works, then?"

"Believe me. I know how this works."

"Good. Good." The therapist ran a hand through his

white hair. It had become thinner over the years. The eyes were the same. Only now they were hidden behind thick glasses.

"I take it you wonder about the way I look. That's okay. Most people do. I usually talk to them about it on their first visit here. Yes, I am an albino. It affects my vision, and I have to be careful when being in the sun. Other than that, I'm perfectly normal. Now, that's about all I will be talking about myself in this room. Let's hear more about you, Alexander. What brings you to my office?"

The man stared at the therapist. He could feel the baton in his pocket, pressing against his leg. He had left the uniform at home today, and only brought the toys.

"It's okay. Take your time. Deciding to see a therapist is a big thing. Opening up and telling your story to a stranger can be hard."

"Oh, I don't mind telling my story; the problem is, you already know it," the man said.

Doctor Korner looked at the man, puzzled. "I'm not sure I quite understand...Have you been here before?"

"No."

"Then, what do you mean? You know what?" the therapist said. "We've gotten off to a bad start. Let's try from the beginning again. Why have you come here to see me?"

The man smiled again, then pulled out the gun and pointed it at the therapist.

"I have come here to kill you."

Dr. Korner gasped and jumped up from the chair. He opened his mouth, trying to scream, but the man moved quickly and grabbed him. He pressed a pair of rolled up socks into his mouth so he couldn't scream. Then, he placed a piece of duct tape over his mouth to keep it in. The therapist screamed, but nothing but muffled sounds came out. He struggled to get out of the man's grip, but had no success. The man pulled away his glasses and stared into the therapist's eyes.

"Take a good look at me. You've seen these eyes before. You've seen these eyes begging you to stop, pleading you to leave them alone, haven't you? Well they're not the ones pleading anymore."

The man forced the therapist to his knees before he pressed the gun to his temple; his hand was shaking in anger. The therapist was sweating heavily and trembling in fear. His eyes appealed for mercy.

I'm not a girl! I'm not a girl. Who am I? The man heard his sister's voice plead in his head.

The man was inclined to simply pull the trigger and finish the therapist right here and now. At least he would never be able to hurt anyone else. But the man had a greater plan for him.

"Now, you listen to me, you asshole. You destroyed my sister's life. Do you know that? You destroyed her. That is why you must die today. That is why I will kill you, but first you have to do as I say. I have a little exercise for you to do. Do you hear me? The faster you do as I tell you, the faster this will be all over, and the less you will suffer. Do you understand me?"

The therapist nodded while trying to speak. He whimpered behind the gag.

"Good. Now, I'll hand you something, and then I'll need you to put it on."

The man opened the backpack while still pointing the gun at Dr. Korner. Looking at him made so many bad memories resurface, and the man's hands were shaking heavily as he pulled out the red dress and black stilettos. He threw both on the floor in front of the therapist.

I'm an alien. Nobody wants me!

"I want you to put this on," the man said, fighting the anger filling him up from all the years of being repeatedly humiliated and tormented.

The therapist whimpered again.

"Take your damn clothes off, now!" the man said harshly, just like the therapist had said to him and Alex so many times.

The therapist started undressing himself. He was crying, the wimp. Probably just trying to appeal to the man's sympathy. But he wasn't going to fall for it.

I'll never be good enough as a girl. I don't know how to be a girl!

"Hurry up!" the man said.

The therapist was now naked, and the man took a picture of him with his phone. Then he told him to put on the dress and the shoes. The therapist did as he was told. The dress was too small, and ripped in places when he tried to put it on. Finally, he succeeded, and the therapist stood in front of the man wearing the beautiful dress and the stilettos. The man smiled. Tears burned in his eyes, thinking about his sister. The man grabbed a mirror from the wall, then placed it in front of the therapist. He used his cell to record a video.

"So, take a look at yourself, dear Doctor," he said. "Then, tell me. Are you a woman?"

The therapist shook his head.

"Are you a man?"

The therapist nodded. The man pulled out his baton, then slammed it across the therapist's face. He made the sound of a buzzer.

"Wrong answer. Try again."

The therapist was on the ground. The baton had left an ugly mark. It was getting swollen.

"Get up and try again," the man said. "Remember, this is an exercise based on your own beliefs. What was it you used to say again? Oh, yes. Gender is learned. Gender is something that can be changed in early childhood. Something like that. Am I right?"

The therapist got up on his knees. The man slapped him with his hand. "Answer me when I speak to you. Wasn't that what you used to say?"

The therapist nodded, while tears ran across his cheeks.

"Good. Now, back to the image you carry of yourself. The image, according to your theories, can be altered with the right influence and exposure to the right things. Tell me once again. Are you a woman?"

The therapist whimpered and looked up at the man.

"Don't look at me, you idiot. Look at the mirror. What do you see? Do you see a woman? Let me put it differently. Do you see a dress?"

The therapist nodded.

"And do we agree that women wear dresses?"

The therapist nodded.

"So, since you are the one wearing the dress that must mean that you are a woman. Am I right?"

The therapist looked up at the man again.

"Right?" the man said.

The therapist nodded.

The man clapped his hands, then lifted the baton up in the air and let it fall as hard as possible on Dr. Korner's head. He fell, forcing him to fall flat to the floor with a thud. Then, he leaned over and whispered, "I'm afraid your time's up."

22

THE INTERVIEW WENT WELL, and Sune and I returned to the newspaper around noon. I wrote my article and we looked at pictures together and chose a series to send over to Jens-Ole. It wasn't a groundbreaking story, but it was fun to do, and it would make a decent article.

I, for one, enjoyed spending time with Sune, even though I did get the feeling that he was eager to get out of there. I wanted to drink coffee with him and discuss the case of the three bodies and how we could dig deeper into the story, but Sune was in a hurry to get out of there.

"I'm sorry, Rebekka, but Jeppe just texted me that he's still at the café, and since I've already done my job here, then…well."

I smiled and kissed him. "That's fine. Go have some fun with your new best friend. Don't forget to pick up the kids, alright?"

"I won't."

"You need me to give you a lift?" I asked.

"Nah. I'll walk. It's pretty close."

"See you later, babe."

I watched as he rushed out the door. Sara pulled off her headphones and looked at me. "Where was he off to in such a hurry?"

"He had plans," I said, and went back behind my desk.

"Oh, by the way," Sara said, picking up a yellow note from the sea of notes and old newspapers flooding her desk. How she ever found anything was beyond my understanding.

"A David Busck called while you were gone." She handed me the note.

I grabbed it and looked at it. My heart pounded in my chest. I had thought a lot about him since yesterday.

"Is that *the* David Busck? As in the incredible hunk that was captured and held prisoner in Syria last year?"

I blushed. I had no idea why. Maybe it was the way she spoke of him. He was really quite handsome. And so sweet.

"Yeah," I said, while trying to avoid Sara's eyes. "It's probably just something work-related. I'll call him later."

I tried to act like I didn't care about it, and put the note casually on my desk. Sara grunted, then returned to her police scanner and put on the headphones. I grabbed my phone and looked at it. It had been silenced during the interview. David had called twice and left a message. I went to the bathroom and listened to it.

"Hi Rebekka. It's me, David. I just wanted to say thank you for yesterday. It was great talking to you again. I really enjoyed it. And I needed it. I have been feeling really bad lately, sleeping poorly and feeling anxious over the smallest things, but talking to you helped me a lot. I feel much better today. I was wondering if I could take you out to lunch today? You're probably working, so…but anyway give me a call when you hear this. Or don't. It's up to you. Bye."

My heart was racing and I couldn't stop smiling as I put the phone down. I exited the restroom, only to find Sara standing right outside. She looked at me suspiciously. "You're usually never this slow," she said. She looked at the phone. "Hm," she grumbled, and walked past me into the restroom.

She made me feel really bad, but I shook it the best I could. If Sune was allowed to have a new best friend, then so was I. As soon as I was back at my desk, I called David.

"Hey, gorgeous. You hungry?"

"I am starving. How about Italian?"

"I know just the place."

23

We met at the restaurant Mama Rosa at one. I hadn't been lying on the phone. I was starving at this point. David was already sitting inside when I entered, and the waiter showed me to the table. I had never been to this restaurant before, but loved the atmosphere. It was small, located on a small secluded street, pulled away from the main street. But, best of all, there was no one else in there. I didn't have to worry about anyone seeing us and telling Sune. It was, after all, a small town, and people started talking very fast. Not that we were doing anything wrong. We were just two friends eating a lunch. After all, Sune was hanging out with his friend as well. I needed someone who understood me just as much as he did.

"So, what's good here?" I asked, when the waiter had handed me the menu.

"I've only been here once, two days ago, but I had the risotto and it was excellent," David said.

"I think I'll try that, then," I said.

David ordered the chicken Parmesan. We both had a beer.

"So, how long are you in town for?" I asked.

David leaned over and smiled. I felt a pinch in my heart.

He was so handsome. His eyes felt like they could see right through me.

"I haven't decided yet," he said.

"Aren't you going back to work?"

"I'm looking into it. I just don't really know what I want, you know what I mean? My priorities have changed. I'm not striving for money and fame anymore. I don't crave being that big journalist anymore. I just want to enjoy my life. I still want to work; I still have to put food on the table, but I'm not as career-minded as I used to be. I'm not sure it's worth it anymore."

"I do know what you mean," I said, and drank from my beer. "I had to leave my job at *Jyllandsposten* a few years ago for the very same reason. I had to get away from my ex-husband, and I knew my daughter was more important than my career. It was tough saying goodbye to my old life, but it's the best thing I've ever done. I love it here."

"I have the biggest respect for that; I really do," David said.

I smiled and drank more from my beer. I looked at his hands and realized even they were handsome. He was just... such a man. I guess that was what I really enjoyed about being with him. He was older than me. He was a real grown-up.

He was everything Sune wasn't.

"The risotto for the lady," the waiter said, as he brought us the food. A hot plate landed in front of me and made me even hungrier than before.

"And the chicken for the gentleman." The waiter looked at us with a smile and clasped hands. "Now, enjoy."

I dug in as soon as the waiter turned around. David laughed. "You weren't kidding when you told me you were starving, were you?"

"No." I spoke with my mouth full, and held a hand up in front of my lips. "I can't remember when I was last this hungry. Lately, my appetite has been kind of nonexistent."

I looked at David, while realizing that I had been feeling better too. I had slept really well for the first time in a long while. And now I was eating too? It was like a cloud had been lifted from my face. Like I was waking up.

"I'm feeling it too," David said. "Spending time with you makes me feel better. It's like all the bad thoughts disappear when you're around."

Could it be? Could it be that David simply made me feel better? That we were somehow good for one another? I couldn't believe it. Maybe I shouldn't feel so guilty about spending time with him. I could choose to look at it as therapy.

"So, how is the case going?" he asked.

"The genderless bodies?" I asked.

I had told David everything about the case the night before.

"Yeah. Any news?"

"Not really. I can't seem to get anywhere with it. I've been thinking about the clothes and the mutilations a lot. I mean, there is definitely a statement of some sort. But what is he trying to tell us?"

"You do know that the pastor was known to be very outspoken against the rights of gays getting married in the church, right?"

"No. I didn't."

"Well, she was. She talked about it in many interviews and in her sermons. She was the only one who refused to marry gays in her church when they said it was allowed."

"So, you're thinking it has something to do with homosexuals? The clothing and the mutilation of their private parts... well, that makes sense. Maybe I should look into that. But why that couple? Tina and Dan Toft were just an ordinary middle-aged couple. Why them?"

David shrugged and sipped his beer. I was getting full now and put the fork down, feeling slightly stuffed.

"I guess that's what we should try and find out," he said.

"We?"

"Yeah. I would like to help you. I don't have much else to do right now, so why not?"

24

DAVID WALKED me back to my office. I felt slightly intoxicated by the entire situation and kept giggling like a schoolgirl at all of his jokes. We looked at store windows and talked about everything and nothing. It was wonderful. So wonderful I felt guilty. When I could see the newspaper's building in the distance, I grabbed my phone from my jacket and looked at it.

I had three missed calls from the office.

"What's wrong?" David asked.

"Something's going on," I said and pressed callback.

Sara sounded agitated. "Where have you been?"

"Out for lunch. The sound on my phone was turned off. What's going on?"

"Dr. Korner has been found killed. They're all over it on the scanner. All officers have been called to the scene."

"I'm on it. Text me the address, and I'll get Sune," I said.

"I've tried him as well. He doesn't answer his phone either. What is wrong with you two these days?" Sara moaned. "I can usually always get ahold of you. At least one of you."

"He's not answering again?" I said angrily. I tried to calm myself. "Doesn't matter. I know where to find him."

I hung up and looked at David. Then I found Sune in my recent calls and called again. Still no answer. I growled and hung up.

"What's going on?" David asked.

"They found another one. Sune is not answering his phone. I don't know what to do. I need a photographer. I don't have time to drive all the way down to the Internet Café to pick him up."

"They found another body?" David asked. "Boy, this guy is busy, huh?"

"You can say that again. Say, didn't you use to do your own photos?" I asked

"Sure. I always work alone. I'm a photojournalist. I can do both. Makes it a lot easier. Why?"

"I think I have one of Sune's cameras in the car. Would you mind helping me out?"

David smiled. "I thought you'd never ask."

We sprang for my car, and I received the text from Sara with the address and a small message about how much she knew. I called Sune again and left a message, telling him I was going on an assignment and to remember pick up the kids today.

"Dr. Korner is apparently some therapist," I told David, as we rushed through town. In the distance, I could hear sirens. "I have to warn you. The last murder scene wasn't pretty; I can tell you that much. I have a feeling this won't be any better."

"I've seen my share of horror scenes when reporting from Syria," he said. "I'll be fine."

"Good. Besides, we're a little late, so we might not get to see much."

The therapist's clinic was located in a small farmhouse outside of town. The surroundings were quiet and would have been idyllic, if it hadn't been for all the police cars and the ambulance parked in the front yard. I spotted my friend, Officer Pedersen, walking out of the building just as we drove up. I waved at him and jumped out. David followed with the camera in his hands. He started shooting pictures right away.

"Rebekka Franck!" Officer Pedersen said and approached us. "Twice in one week. I can hardly believe my luck."

I pretended to be flattered and smiled. "So, what happened here? Is it related to the three other killings?"

"You know I can't say anything. We've all been told to keep quiet about this case."

"Ah, okay," I said, sounding disappointed. "But you can tell us who it was, right? Can you confirm the victim was Dr. Korner?"

Officer Pedersen looked at me, then looked around to see if anyone had seen us talking. Everyone seemed too busy to care. He pulled us to the side. "Yes. I can tell you it *was* Dr. Korner. I can tell you he *was* killed. I can also tell you who found him. Would that do? But you didn't get it from me, alright?"

"That would be perfect," I said.

"It was his secretary," Officer Pedersen said. "She walked in and found him."

I noted the name in my notebook, and as I thanked the officer and he turned to walk away, I suddenly stopped him.

"Excuse me?"

"Yes?"

"You're missing your baton, Officer."

He felt his belt. "Yes, you're right. I must have forgotten it in my car. Silly, huh?"

I smiled. "Very."

25

WE FOUND THE SECRETARY, Miss Nielsen, at her apartment in downtown Karrebaeksminde. We had to have Sara help us out, since all Officer Pedersen gave us was her name. I called Sara and asked her if she could help us find the address, hoping that she would be able to somehow look her up online, but there was no need to.

"I know Sandra," she said. "She lives right downtown above SunTan, the sun tanning place. "I'll text you the exact address. I'll call her and ask her if she'll want to do the interview."

It was that easy. I thanked God for having Sara, and then waited for her to call back. It took less than five minutes.

"She'll see you. I have to warn you, though. She's pretty shaken up. She's been interrogated over and over by the police until they finally drove her home less than half an hour ago. But she has agreed to talk to you. Just make it short, okay?"

"Got it."

I looked at my watch. It was getting late. I hoped Sune had

picked up the kids by now. He would have to make dinner as well. I texted him.

STILL ON JOB. IT'S GOING TO BE LATE.

That was it. I'd have to fill him in later.

Sandra Nielsen looked pretty bad when she opened the door to her apartment and let us in. Her eyes were swollen and her hand shaking badly when I shook it.

"Let's go in the living room," she said, and we followed her. "Help yourselves to some coffee in the kitchen, if you like. I'm sorry if I'm not much of a host."

"That's fine," David said. "I'll grab some for all of us."

He left and came back with three cups. Sandra's hands could hardly hold onto hers when she tried to lift it. She sniffled and wiped her nose on a napkin.

"We won't stay long," I said. "First of all, I would like to say I'm so sorry for what happened to your boss. How long did you work for him?"

"Ah, let me see," Sandra said and sniffled again. "It feels like forever. Twenty years? Yeah, it'll be twenty years this summer. Wow. I didn't even realize it had been that long."

I wrote it on my pad. "Time sure flies. So, tell me what happened today? I know you've been through this with the police, but I would be very grateful if you would repeat it for our readers."

"I'll be taking some photos while you talk," David said. "Will that be okay?"

Sandra chuckled. "Oh, I'm such a mess." She corrected her hair and wiped her nose again. "Well, I guess it'll be alright."

"So, tell me what happened today?"

"It was a day like any other. I mean, Dr. Korner had clients like he always has. There was nothing unusual. He had a new one at one o'clock. He seemed like a nice guy. He went in and they started their session. I...I never even heard a thing. Well, the rooms are pretty insulated; it's kind of the idea that no one is supposed to hear what goes on in there, what they talk about, right? So, I guess that's why I didn't hear anything, but still. I mean..."

Sandra stopped and picked up another napkin. Tears had started rolling across her cheeks. She looked at the ceiling, trying to hold them back. "Oh it's just...I mean, when you work with someone for this long..."

"You cared about him," David said in between photos. "That's only natural."

"I mean, he could be a prick sometimes. A real bastard, and I didn't always agree with his ideas or his methods, especially in the earlier years, but what do I know about anything? I'm just a secretary, right?"

"So, what happened? A new patient arrived; can you describe him?" I asked.

"Well, I thought I could, but the police told me he was wearing a wig and thick glasses that they later found in the garbage outside the clinic. But I do know he was tall and quite handsome. I still believe I would be able to recognize him if I saw him again, at least I hope I would. But I do remember he was wearing a blue jacket and had a backpack with him. A blue and red EastPak."

"So, this patient, did he leave afterwards?" I asked, while writing everything she said on my pad.

"Yes. When time was up, he came out of the office. I asked him if we should schedule another appointment, and he said he would call when he had his calendar, then he smiled, waved at me, and left. There was nothing odd about his behavior. He seemed to be in a hurry to get out, but that's not unusual. People often feel a little embarrassed coming out, especially if they've cried or something. It's only natural to want to get away in a hurry. So, I didn't take much notice of it."

"So, what did you do after he left?" I asked. I sensed my

phone was vibrating in my pocket, but ignored it. It had to wait.

"Usually, Dr. Korner brings out the patient's files when he's done with them, and I put them back and hand him the next patient's files. So, I was waiting for him to come out, but when he didn't, I walked in."

"And what did you see?"

Sandra Nielsen started crying again. David handed her another Kleenex. "Take your time," he said.

"He…he…" Sandra sniffled, then looked at me. "The first I saw were his legs. They were dangling in the air. I couldn't believe my eyes. Dr. Korner was hanging from the ceiling, a rope around his neck, dressed in…Well, that was the odd part. He was dressed in women's clothes. A red dress and black stilettos. He even had make-up on." Sandra broke down and cried harder. "Who would do such a thing?"

"Do you know if the doctor had any enemies?" I asked.

She shook her head with a sob, crying.

"You said you didn't always agree with his theories and methods, what did you mean by that?" I asked.

"Well, that was mostly back in the days when I just started working for him. He had this idea, him and the doctor he worked with back then. They believed that gender could be reversed. That it was something that was taught at an early age and not something you were born with. That it could be somehow reassigned with the right influences during childhood."

"What?" I blurted out. It sounded so strange.

"It was back in the nineties. Dr. Korner and Dr. Winter worked with a lot of kids. You know boys that dressed up like girls and the other way around. Kids that believed they were born in the wrong body."

"You mean transgender?" I asked.

She sniffled again before she sipped her coffee. "Yes.

Parents would come to them and ask them to help their kids. Mostly because they didn't want them to think they were born in the wrong body. Because they wanted their little boy to act more like a boy."

"You're kidding me, right?" I asked.

She shook her head. "I'm afraid not. They had this very serious research going on. Got money from the state and everything. I never liked the project much, but I'm not the one with all the degrees."

"Well, I guess that would explain the woman's outfit, then," David said.

"You mean someone's angry about what they did?" I asked. "I guess that is a motive. But you say you've never seen this patient before?"

"I don't think so. His name was Alexander, Alexander Hansen. I didn't recognize the name, but now that you say it, there was something vaguely familiar about him. I just can't figure out what."

"Maybe he's an old patient of Dr. Korner's?" David asked. "From when he was a child?"

"Do you really think so?" she asked. "That's a terrible thought."

"Do you have the journals from back then?" I asked. "Maybe we could find his name in there?"

She shook her head. "We only save them for five years. We can't keep everything."

"Of course not," I said.

My phone kept vibrating in my pocket, and I finally pulled it out. The display said it was from William's day-care mom.

"I'm sorry. I have to get this," I said, and picked it up with my heart racing in my chest. "This is Rebekka."

"It's five-thirty, Rebekka," she said from the other end. "I close at five."

"Oh, my God. Sune didn't pick up William?"

26

I WAS SO angry I was shaking as I drove towards the day-care and picked up William. I made a million excuses to Anette, and she told me not to worry about it, just never do it again. The worst part was going to the school and picking up Tobias and Julie. The school had also tried to call me several times, and the lady in the aftercare looked at me very angrily, even after my million excuses. She wasn't as forgiving as Anette.

"I have a life too, you know," she said. "I have my own kids to go home to."

It was so embarrassing.

"I'm so, so sorry. It'll never happen again. I promise," I said, but I could tell she didn't believe me. I knew every aftercare experienced the moms that were always too late to pick up their kids, and now she thought I was one of them. I could tell by the way she looked at me. I had been stigmatized.

"I thought you wouldn't come, Mom," Julie declared, as soon as we were in the car. William was crying helplessly, and Julie was on the verge of breaking down as well. I cursed Sune and part of me hoped he was hurt or something. It would be the only excuse I would accept at this point.

But I had a feeling he wasn't. And the thought drove me nuts. I kept calling his cell, but got no answer. I reached the point where I was actually worried about him and wondering if something really serious might have happened.

I drove like crazy through town, shifting between being furious and deeply concerned. Neither was a comfortable feeling.

"I will always come and pick you up, sweetheart. I was just a little late, that's all," I said to comfort them. "I lost track of time."

"Where is my dad?" Tobias asked. "Couldn't he have picked us up?"

You'd think, wouldn't you?

I parked in the driveway, then shooed the children out of the car. Julie hugged me on her way out.

"Don't ever forget me," she said.

I looked into her blue eyes. "I won't, sweetie. You know that. And I promise to never be this late again."

It was with petrified steps that I walked up to the house. The front door was locked, and I fumbled with the keys before finally opening it.

"Sune?" I almost screamed.

Where the hell is he? Has something bad happened to him?

There was no answer. I ran into the living room, but it was empty. I stomped upstairs and found my dad in his bed, reading a magazine.

"Hey, honey. Say, is all well? You look pale."

"I can't find Sune. He didn't pick up the kids from school. Has he been home at all?"

"He was here earlier. I heard him come home around one o'clock. He came in here and asked me if I needed anything. Later, I fell asleep, and when I woke up it was all quiet downstairs. Until you guys all came home. Is it that late?"

"It's past six o'clock," I said.

"Oh, my goodness. Well, it gets dark so early these days, I lose complete track of time."

"Yeah. Well, could you stay with the kids while I go look for him?" I asked. "I'll make some sandwiches for them to eat, so they won't be too hungry."

"Sure. I'll come down in a minute."

"Thanks, Dad."

I closed the door to his room with my heart pounding. Where could Sune be? Had something really happened to him? I tried calling him again, but no answer. I ran downstairs to the kitchen and made a bunch of ham sandwiches, and soon my dad came down. He looked better.

"Are you sure you're up for this?" I asked and kissed his cheek. "I hope it won't be long."

"Yes, of course I am," he said.

"I'll take William, so you only need to keep an eye on the big ones. I'll be home as soon as I can."

My dad grabbed my arm and looked me in the eyes. "We'll be fine. Sune is fine too. Worry will give you nothing but an ulcer. It's like a rocking-chair, remember?"

I nodded. "I know. It keeps me busy but gets me nowhere." I smiled and kissed him. Then I grabbed William, gave him a sandwich and a juice box, and headed out the door.

As I opened the front door, I spotted Sune further down the street riding his bike. Next to him was Jeppe on his bike. They were both laughing and chatting loudly. My heart dropped, and I stood like I was frozen on the front step. Could this really be? I mean, I felt relieved that nothing had happened to him, but it was very quickly replaced by extreme fury.

What the hell had happened to him?

They came closer, and now Sune was waving at me. Jeppe did the same. Had they no idea what had happened? And that was when I saw it. I couldn't believe my eyes at first. It freaked me out.

Jeppe had gotten a Mohawk. The exact same as Sune's. He was even wearing the same spiked leather band around his neck.

He looked exactly like Sune.

27

"Doesn't he look great?" Sune asked, as they came closer. "Jeppe told me he loved the way I looked, so we took a trip around town, went to my hairdresser and shopped for some clothes, giving him the same look. The hairdresser gave Jeppe a short Mohawk and shaved the sides of his head, then fixed mine up to match."

Sune looked great. I liked the short Mohawk, but I was so angry I couldn't even speak. I simply couldn't get a word across my lips. And not only that. I felt hurt as well. I felt abandoned.

"What?" Sune asked. "You look angry."

Do you have any idea what time it is?" I asked. I knew I sounded like his mother, but what the heck was I supposed to say?

"I know. We lost track of time," he said.

I had to really hold it in to not explode. "You lost track of time? What about the kids?"

He looked confused. "I thought you were going to pick them up?" Sune said. "You said so when I left the office earlier.

You said you were done with the article, so you could pick them up."

"What? No, I didn't. I asked you to pick them up. Don't you remember?"

Sune shook his head. "No you didn't. I specifically remember you said you would pick them up."

I couldn't believe this. Had he completely lost it? "I didn't. And I couldn't pick them up. There was another story. I texted you. I called you. Why don't you pick up your phone anymore?"

"I think I'd better head home," Jeppe said. "See you later, Sune." They gave each other a fist bump and the hairs on the back of my neck rose when I realized how much they suddenly looked alike. It was kind of eerie.

"I'm sorry," Sune said. He sounded like he was getting angry now. "My phone ran out of battery. I didn't have a charger. What do you expect me to do?"

I closed my eyes for a second, then put William down and let him run back inside the house.

The important part is that no one got hurt. Everyone is well.

"I'm serious here, Rebekka. You can't expect to be able to reach me at all times. Sometimes I don't hear my phone; sometimes it runs out of battery. It's just what happens. It's not something I planned."

"I know. I know. It's just that…well, the kids were picked up too late. I thought you were picking them up. I left you a message on your voice mail and texted you. I assumed you had seen it. I…I don't know how to react to this. If I can't trust you to be there for me, I don't know how I can do my job. I need to know that I can count on you, and that you don't just disappear for long periods of time. We're supposed to be a team here."

Sune nodded. "I know. And I believe we are. But every now and then, I need to be me as well. I need to be able to go out with a friend. I can't have you controlling me constantly, acting like you're my mother."

I bit my lip and looked at him. It didn't sound like Sune. "Where is all this coming from all of a sudden?"

He rolled his eyes. "Ah, come on," he said. "You really don't think I'm capable of having an opinion of my own? You really don't have good thoughts about me, do you? You emasculate me. Make me feel like a child. Jeppe was right about everything. To think I defended you when he said those things."

Sune sighed, shook his head, and walked past me. I stood in the cold for a few seconds, wondering what had happened to the man I loved, the man I thought I shared a life with. In just a few days, he had completely changed.

I felt a deep sadness spread inside of me as I turned around and followed him inside, where the kids were fighting over a toy in the living room. I grabbed William and went upstairs. I gave him a bath. Then I took him to his room. I read a story and sang a song, then sang three others, until he was finally satisfied and fell asleep. I sat in the darkness of his room, wondering if I should even bother to go downstairs, or if I should simply just go to bed right away. I really didn't want to spend time with my family. I didn't feel like fighting more with Sune or have to solve any more conflicts. I wondered what had happened to Julie and Tobias. They used to be the best of friends when Sune and I simply worked together. Ever since we moved in together, everything had changed. It was like they felt they had to constantly compete about everything. Was it an age thing? Or was the moving in together simply bad for them?

Was it bad for us?

28

It was putting it mildly to say that school was terrible for the twins. Mostly for Alex, of course. Upon entering kindergarten, she became the object of instant ridicule from classmates, both male and female. When she walked by, they would giggle behind her back, while whispering and pointing fingers. And it was everybody. Not just a few mean students. And not just on some days. It was every day. Non-stop. They called her names, ignored her, and didn't include her in anything.

Even their teacher didn't accept her, the man recalled. The teacher knew something was different about her.

The man could so vividly remember all those disapproving looks, the glares, the name-calling, and even the teacher who would simply point Alex out in class, call her up when he knew she wouldn't be able to answer, or ridicule her in class, only to make all the other students feel like it was okay to mock her. It became something everyone did, and that somehow made it legal.

Even the man knew that there was something wrong with his sister. Of course he did. There are certain ways people are expected to act and be. As a boy, you know what a girl is supposed to be like. Girls are delicate. They're supposed to be into girl-stuff, dolls and tea parties and princesses and stuff. Alex wasn't like that. She liked to do boy-stuff. And Alex even knew it herself. She looked at the girls playing and wondered why she didn't want to do the things they did, why she wasn't interested in what they played, then looked at the boys and saw that they looked completely different than she. Soon, she started seeing herself as not belonging in either category, and started referring to herself as an *it*.

In school, her teacher thought she was dumber than the rest, and had her tested, but the test only proved that she was within the normal intelligence range, and therefore, the teacher concluded that because of her malfunctioning in the classroom, she had to be held back. She was simply unwilling to submit to authority.

Knowing this, their parents contacted Dr. Winter, who told the school that there was nothing wrong with Alex, and that they had to consider her fragile emotional state, but that she was perfectly fit for first grade. Only a few weeks into first grade, however, the teacher had to file a report on Alex stating that she did *everything opposite of what was expected of her.*

After that, Dr. Winter intensified his exercises with Alex, and often asked her and her brother to come to the clinic alone without their parents. That's where they learned that there were two sides to Dr. Winter. The one he showed when their parents were around and the one he showed when they were alone. He would undress them and have them examine their body parts, to make sure Alex could see that there was an anatomical difference between the two of them. He would show them pictures of naked grown-up people in strange positions, often sexual positions, and ask Alex what she liked, who she could see herself having sexual relations with.

Every time, she would point to the girl. After that, Dr. Winter concluded that Alex was a lesbian and explained that to their parents. But their parents never accepted that fact. They turned to the pastor for help. The pastor told them to whip the child, to force her out of it. The pastor called it a disease that could only be held down with brutal force. With time, she would learn to accept the fact that she was a girl and that she was supposed to marry a boy like all normal girls.

But she didn't. Alex refused to accept it.

Night after night, she still cried in her sleep, stating that she was a boy, that she wasn't a girl, that she would never be a girl.

When puberty hit, Dr. Winter started having more and more sessions with them both. He talked constantly about sex and showed them pornographic movies and pictures to the extent that they started fearing having to go there. They would scream and yell every time their parents told them it was time for their session with the doctor or the therapist.

When Alex's breasts still hadn't developed at the age of fourteen, Dr. Winter started giving her estrogen.

"To make you fill out a bra," he said.

Alex was angry and refused to take the pills. "I don't want to wear a bra," she yelled, and then ran to her room. But her parents forced the pills in her anyway.

The mocking continued at school, and every day, Alex's stomach hurt so badly while walking the long way to the school.

Until one day, when Alex spotted Leonora. She was a new girl in eighth grade. Tall and blond and simply gorgeous.

The man sighed and looked at the old class photos. He let a finger run across Leonora's picture. They had both been in love with her back then, but she was Alex's great love, so the man had stayed away. Finally, Alex had found something to be excited about, something to make her day brighter. Finally, she actually looked forward to going to school. Finally, she was smiling. It was like a spell had been broken, like a curse had been lifted on her life.

The man shed a tear when thinking about it. He looked at the picture of the beautiful blond girl that had made his sister so happy for the first time in her short life. That smile, the long blond hair and the blue eyes were looking back at him. He kept touching her face, first gently, then harder and harder, rubbing on the picture with his nail, until he scraped the face off.

29

"If a serial killer is on the loose, then we need to warn people."

I was sitting in the office the next day, wondering about the four killings and how they were connected when Jens-Ole called. I told him I thought it might be the same killer.

"We need to tell the story, Rebekka," he said. "So people are careful and don't go out late at night and so on. They deserve to know."

"It's just...well, I can't get anyone from inside the police force to publicly make a statement. I can't get it documented that the killings are connected. When I call and ask about it, they tell me they can't say anything yet. But I looked at the autopsy reports, and all of them have been beaten with a weapon similar to a police baton. They all conclude that. Even the last one, Dr. Korner. The baton leaves marks on the skin. This guy is beating his victims to death, then dressing them up and displaying them for us to find."

"But you can't write that because you got the information illegally, and the police are denying and covering it up because it might be one of their own, which makes it even more urgent for us to tell the story," Jens-Ole grumbled. "What do we do? Hm…"

"Unnamed sources? Anonymous?" I asked, looking at Sara, who placed a piece of pastry in front of me and a cup of coffee. I smiled and mouthed a thank you while she went back to the police scanner.

"I hate having to do that," Jens-Ole said. "It's just not credible enough. It sounds like we're guessing and making up our own stories, but yes, I believe that's what we'll have to do. It's the only way. You do that, and I'll take care of management. Write, Goddammit. Write your story."

He hung up. I put the phone down and looked at Sune, who was staring at his screen. We had hardly spoken since last night. I had asked him to come in and help me get access to the police file on Dr. Korner, so I could check the forensic report. Now, there was nothing more for him to do, and I knew he was only waiting for me to tell him he could go home, but I didn't want to. I knew he would only spend time with that creepy guy Jeppe, and I hated that. I knew it was selfish, but I wanted him to stay here with me. After all, the newspaper was paying him for an entire day. They had to. Even if we only asked him to do a little work, as a freelancer he was being paid for the entire day. So, while eating my pastry, I wondered if I could come up with something else for him to do. I was, after all, writing a big article about how the killings were connected, and they needed some photos besides the ones they already had.

"Sune could you maybe go downtown and take some pictures from outside the police station for my article?" I asked.

"Why can't your journalist friend do it?" he asked.

Sune had been mad at me ever since he realized David had taken the pictures for my story the day before.

"Oh, I'm sorry, your *photo*-journalist friend," he corrected himself sarcastically.

"Could you please just do this for me?" I asked, ignoring his comments. I wasn't in the mood for fighting.

"Can't you just take some pictures from the archives? The building is the exact same as it was the last time."

"You know they prefer the pictures to be new," I said.

Sune shrugged. Then he grabbed his camera. "I guess," he said.

Sara took off her headset. "Could you bring back lunch? Maybe some of those sandwiches from the bakery on the corner? They're so good."

Sune shrugged again. "I guess." He put his jacket on, and without a word of goodbye, he left the office.

"What's eating him?" Sara asked when he had left.

I sighed and leaned back in my chair. I had a bad feeling inside of me. I didn't like what was happening between us.

"A late teenage rebellion?" I said.

Sara laughed out loud while putting her headphones back on. I didn't laugh.

30

I DIDN'T like the idea of writing an article without anyone confirming its content, and luckily, after writing most of it, I had an idea. I called an old friend at the Copenhagen forensic department. I knew him when I was in Iraq. He worked on helping identify victims, especially when a bomb had been set off in a public marketplace or after a roadside bomb attack. He came back to Denmark a year after me.

"Rebekka! Wow. It's been years. How have you been?" Kim asked.

"Good. Can't complain. Guess you heard I moved to Karrebaeksminde?"

"Yes. Yes, I heard. Terrible story with Peter, huh? I guess he really lost it after we came home, huh? I'm so sorry for you, Rebekka. You seemed like such a great couple."

"Well, things are not always as they seem," I said.

"So, what can I do for you?" he asked.

"I need a favor."

"I believe I owe you one for that time in Baghdad when you saved me from that bomb. I guess I owe you several. You saved my life, Rebekka. I'll do anything for you."

"I need you to do something now. And it's a big request."

"Okay. Let's hear it," he said.

"I want you to comment on an article I'm writing about four killings here in Karrebaeksminde. I believe they're all connected; I believe it's the same killer, but I can't get it confirmed."

Kim went quiet. "I know what you're talking about. I think I could do that. I mean, the management won't like it, since we're not supposed to talk about the case to the press, but for you, I'll do it for you."

"Really? You have no idea how happy I am. What I need is for you to tell me the similarities in the cases."

"I can do that. I mean, it's bound to get out somehow anyway, right?"

"I will tell the story no matter what," I said. "I just prefer to have my facts confirmed."

"Naturally. You're a professional. Always have been," he said.

"One more thing," I said. "I need you to confirm for me what the murder weapon is."

Kim went quiet once again. I could tell he was thinking. "That's going to be a little harder," he said.

"I know it was a police-baton, so I'll write it anyway," I said.

Kim sighed. "This is going to be ugly," he said. "But if you ask me about it, then I guess I can't lie."

I smiled and looked at Sara, who could tell something was going on. I gave her a thumbs up and she smiled back.

I spoke with Kim for about an hour on the phone, getting all my details confirmed, and even the murder weapon. Then I thanked him and hung up. I texted Jens-Ole and told him the article was now confirmed and almost done. I looked at the clock and realized Sune had been gone for a long time. I wondered if there was a line at the bakery, then returned to my article, not thinking anymore about it. I went to the kitchen and poured myself some more coffee, which I drank while finishing the story. I sent it to Sara and had her read through it to make sure it was clear, and that I hadn't left anything out.

"It's really good," she said when she was done. "Kind of scared me. To think there's a policeman out there beating people to death with his baton. Made me shiver."

I was satisfied with her reaction, and wanted to send the article, but I still needed Sune's pictures. I looked at the clock and wondered what was taking him so long. I grabbed my phone and looked at the display. He hadn't tried to call or text me. I decided to call him. He picked up.

"Where are you?" I asked.

"What, are you checking up on me now?" he asked. "You're not my mother, remember?"

"Well, I'm sorry if that's the way you feel, but I was a little worried and wanted to know if you had run into trouble."

"As a matter of fact, I did run into someone," he said. "I ran into Henrik Pedersen outside the station. I talked to him for a long time, and he told me he could confirm that they were looking within the police force for the killer. I took his picture and wrote his quote down for your article."

Oh, my God!

"Are you serious?"

"Deadly serious."

"That's awesome, Sune."

"Well, I did have to smooth-talk him for a little while, but I got the feeling he liked the idea of being in the paper and having his photo in it."

"That's so great, Sune. Thank you so much. Now my article will be complete."

"You're very welcome."

"So, are you on your way back?" I asked.

"Well, I'm kind of on my way downtown to meet up with Jeppe at the Internet Café. We wanted to play a few games. I can send the pictures and the quote from there if you like. I really don't need to come in for that."

My heart dropped. I missed hanging out with Sune. I wanted to have lunch with him. I wanted to discuss the story like we used to do.

"Well…I guess not."

"Great. I'll send everything to you in the drop box. See you later."

31

LEONORA AND ALEX soon became the closest of friends in the entire school. The man remembered vividly how they would stick together in everything. Even finishing each other's sentences from time to time like an old married couple. He couldn't help feeling a little jealous of them, since he didn't have anyone that close in his life. He had always been the one closest to his sister, and he also had a secret crush on Leonora. But he never told anyone how he felt. Because, at the same time, he was happy for them. He was thrilled for Alex. And finally the screaming and crying at night had ceased.

Their parents still tried to change her ways and force her to wear girls' clothes. They refused to cut her hair like she wanted them to, and told her she would be pulled out of school and be homeschooled if she ever did it herself. So, Alex looked like a girl on the outside, with her long black hair and black dresses, but she never acted like one. Her every movement, even the expressions on her face, were masculine. It made her look odd and made her classmates continue to tease her.

But now, she had someone in her life. Leonora, the prettiest girl in the entire school, suddenly stood up for her. She would tell people off and get them to back down. And Alex was in love from the very first day. She would follow Leonora everywhere she went and do anything the girl told her to.

Their parents thought Alex had finally gotten a real friend, and that she was now, at long-last, accepting the fact that she was actually a girl and behaving like one. So, they applauded this new person in Alex's life. They invited her over and drove Alex to the mall when Leonora wanted to meet her there.

What they didn't know was that their daughter secretly dreamt about her new best friend at night in ways they would never have accepted if they had known.

But her brother knew. He listened to her when she spoke about Leonora and saw the sparkle in her eyes. He knew how much Alex wanted to be close to Leonora, but he also feared deeply for the day when Leonora figured out how her best friend felt. How she secretly desired her.

"You don't know if Leonora likes girls," he said one night, trying to break it to his sister gently.

Alex looked at him like he was a complete idiot. "I'm not a girl," she said.

"Yes, you are," he argued. "Look at you. Look at your hair, your clothes, your breasts."

Alex looked down. "Those are not mine," she said. "They came from the pills, remember? I never wanted them. And the hair and clothes? That doesn't make me a girl."

"Okay, but the fact that you have a vagina must be proof enough, right? I mean, how much clearer does it get?"

Alex looked at her brother through the dark almost black hair that was always hanging in front of her face. Then she growled.

"I'm not a girl! I'm not a girl!"

"Yes, you are!"

For the first time in their life as twins, Alex lost her

temper. She grabbed her brother around his neck and started choking him.

"Say I'm a boy. Say I'm a boy!" she yelled forcefully.

The brother was terrified that she was going to strangle him. She held him so tightly around the neck, it hurt like crazy, and he couldn't breathe. He gasped and spurted for air.

"Say it!"

The boy felt how he started to lose consciousness, while he struggled to stay alive, when the door to their room opened and their parents stormed in.

"What's going on here?"

Seeing what was happening, their father sprang for Alex and pulled her away from her brother, who lay for a long time on the bed gasping for air and coughing. He still remembered Alex's scream as they carried her out of the room.

"I'm not a girl! Say I'm not a girl!"

32

When I was done with my article and had chosen a few of Sune's pictures to send along with it, I picked up all the kids and went home. I hadn't heard anything from Sune, and as time passed, I wondered if he was even going to make it home for dinner.

My dad came down and sat at the table while I made Danish meatballs, *frikadeller,* and baked potatoes. He looked tired and pale, and I wondered when he had last been outside to get some fresh air.

"I'll open the window," he would always say, when I told him fresh air would do him good.

I wondered if I should take him out for a walk when Sune got back and could look after the kids. Even if it was dark out, he would still get some air. It was always hard in the wintertime for him to get outside because he was afraid of slipping. The sidewalks were icy and he could easily fall. I couldn't blame him.

"So, what's going on with you and Sune these days?" he asked.

I shrugged, while cutting the lettuce for the salad. "I really don't know. It's like he prefers to spend time with that Jeppe guy more than me. I guess I can't blame him. I'm not exactly all fun like him. I'm older; I have more responsibility. I don't like spending all day playing video games. It's just a waste of time, if you know what I mean."

My dad chuckled. I poured him a glass of wine. The doctor had said one glass a day would be good for his heart. I poured one for myself and sipped it. I felt the sadness spread, thinking about how it always used to be Sune that I shared my wine with. We would laugh and talk about our day or a story we worked on, or laugh at the crazy kids.

"It's like half of me is missing, somehow. I mean, we used to do everything together, and now he's off having fun with someone else. I don't mind him having fun, that's not the problem…"

"But you would prefer that he had fun with you," my dad said.

"That's how it used to be."

I sipped my wine again when my phone vibrated. Hoping it was Sune, I picked it up. It was a text.

HOW WAS YOUR DAY?

It was from David. I sighed and rubbed my forehead. Why did I feel so happy when hearing from him? That wasn't how it was supposed to be. I texted back, trying to stay professional and only talk about work:

GOOD. GOT A BIG ARTICLE IN FOR TOMORROW. DON'T MISS IT.

He texted me back:

I WON'T. I ONLY MISS YOU.

I looked at the text, then put the phone down. It was getting dangerous now. Did I have feelings for him? Why was I happy that he sent that? Why did I want to put everything down and go see him? Why had I missed him all day?

The phone vibrated again. I picked it up. But this time it

wasn't from David. It was a text from an unknown number. It said:

NICE SHIRT, REBEKKA.

I looked at the text, feeling baffled. What was this? Who was it? I shook my head and put the phone down, when it vibrated again.

RED IS MY FAVORITE COLOR.

I stared at the text, feeling my heart race in my chest. Who the hell was this person? How did he know what I was wearing? Had he seen me earlier today? Was he looking at me right now?

I stared at the dark windows. It was pitch-black outside. Someone was walking his dog, and it was peeing on the streetlamp. Other than that, the street was empty. I looked at the text again. Then I wrote back.

WHO IS THIS?

I put the phone down and went back to making my salad when the phone vibrated again. I picked it up.

LITTLE BOY UNSEEN

"What?" I asked out loud. What was that supposed to mean?

"What's wrong?" My dad asked and looked up from the paper he was reading.

I shook my head and put the phone in my pocket. "Nothing." I forced a smile, and hoped he wouldn't notice how upset I was.

"Well, I don't think we can wait for Sune any longer," I said. "The kids are starving. Let's eat."

33

Sune didn't come home until the middle of the night. I had just fallen asleep after hours of staring at the ceiling, wondering where he was and what he was doing. I heard the door open and then the bed moved as he climbed in. It woke me up.

"Where were you?" I asked, knowing I once again sounded like his mother, but also feeling that I had a right to know.

"With Jeppe."

"You smell like beer."

"Well, we had a couple and played some pool. Is that a problem?" Sune asked, sounding drowsy.

I cleared my throat and decided not to ask any more questions. I wanted to talk to him about what they had been up to. I wanted to know if they had been looking at girls, or maybe even talking to them. I wanted to ask about everything and maybe yell a little at him for abandoning me like this, but I didn't have the strength. Besides, Sune was drunk, and I wouldn't be able to talk sense with him.

It had to wait.

"No," I said instead. "Let's get some sleep."

Soon after, Sune snored, while I couldn't fall back to sleep. I stared at the ceiling and out of the window for hours before sleep finally overpowered me.

The next morning, I could hardly drag myself out of bed. I let Sune sleep in, mostly because I didn't want to bother discussing anything with him, or even looking at him. I just wanted to get the kids ready for school, and then get myself to the office. I made breakfast for everyone and served some for my dad on a tray. When everyone was ready, we left the house without even saying goodbye to Sune. I told Tobias that his dad was still sleeping and that he had come home late.

At the office, Jens-Ole had called to congratulate me on the big article that had made the front cover of the newspaper this morning.

"And I heard Sune landed the officer. You two make quite the team," he said joyfully.

"Well, I don't know about that. We try our best."

"So, do you have any follow-up leads for today?"

"Not yet," I said. "I was thinking about getting someone to tell me how easy it is to get ahold of a police-baton and how common they are."

"Sounds really good. Even though the police-killer angle is a good—and scary—one, we need to cover all aspects. You're answering the question everyone is left with. Is this a police-killer, or could someone else have done it? Very good, my dear, very good. Let me know what you come up with. I was also thinking about doing a vox-pop with people in the area, asking them if they were afraid and if they are taking any precautions, you know...get the mood of the population. That's always popular."

I sighed. I hated vox-pops. It was so populist. Just going into the street and asking random people how they felt about something. In a case like this, it only added to the fear in the population, and I didn't like that much. I believed they should know what was going on, but not be scared to walk the streets. But if my editor wanted me to do this, there was no way around it.

"Sure. I'll do that a little later," I said.

"That's my girl."

We hung up, and I looked at Sara.

"You look like you could use a day off," she said.

"I didn't sleep well last night."

"Trouble in paradise?"

I stared at my screen, while her question lingered in my mind. There was no use in trying to hide it anymore, was there?

"I guess you could say that," I said.

"I figured. It'll get better," she said.

"I sure hope it will."

"Trying to play family is a lot harder than just dating," she said with a smile.

She had no idea how right she was.

34

Under Leonora's protection, the bullying stopped for some months for Alex. Every now and then, someone would say something, but only to be told off by Leonora, and with her being the most popular girl in school, they would immediately stop.

Unfortunately, Leonora soon became bored with Alex and started having new friends to hang out with. It was a source of frustration for Alex, who struggled with increasing jealousy. She still clung very close to Leonora, and for a long time, she managed to keep her to herself. But Leonora was getting tired of the staring eyes in the cafeteria and the many whispering voices behind their backs. In the beginning, it had been fun to take Alex under her wing, to surprise everyone and take in the one that no one wanted. It had been fun. And she would probably have kept Alex close for a longer time if it hadn't been for that one night in December when they had been in Leonora's room, listening to the latest CD from The Cure that Alex had bought for her.

They were both lying on their backs on Leonora's bed, talking about their dreams for the future.

"I want to be a rock-star," Leonora said. "I want to travel the world and not be stuck in this small town."

Alex laughed. "I bet you'd be a great rock-star. Everybody would love you."

"You love me, don't you, Alex?" Leonora had suddenly said.

Alex hadn't known what to say. Thinking she might as well be honest she said, "Well…yes. Yes, I do."

With her heart pounding in her chest, Alex had waited for Leonora's answer, wondering what she was thinking, wondering how she would react.

She's going to hate me. She's going to tell me she'll never see me again…that I am no longer her friend.

But that wasn't how she reacted. Not at all.

"Would you like to kiss me?" Leonora said instead. She turned her head and looked intensely at Alex.

Alex stared at her lips. Her beautiful soft lips. Oh, how she had dreamt of kissing those lips. How she had longed to know what it would be like to kiss them. But she hesitated. Alex didn't feel sure if Leonora really meant it. She was, after all, her best friend.

Leonora pushed her shoulder playfully and laughed. "Come on, Alex. I know you want to. Everyone at school tells me you're a lesbian and that you only hang out with me because you're in love with me. Don't lie to me. It's okay. You can be honest with me. You can trust me. I am your best friend."

Alex blushed and looked down at the bed, avoiding Leonora's eyes.

"You do want to kiss me, don't you?" Leonora asked again.

Alex looked up and their eyes locked. Then, she smiled. "Yes," she said.

"Yes what?"

"Yes, I want to kiss you, Leonora."

Leonora laughed and sat up. "I knew it!"

Alex shrugged, feeling self-confident, but still hopeful that maybe, just maybe Leonora felt the same way.

Leonora closed her eyes and stuck out her lips. "Then kiss me, you fool!"

Alex blushed again. She felt a deep sensation in her stomach, while waves of excitement rushed over her. Could this really be happening?

"What are you waiting for?" Leonora said.

Alex shrugged, then leaned over and closed her eyes, just before her lips hit Leonora's. She could smell her skin. It was intoxicating. She held her breath as her lips landed on Leonora's. But something was wrong. Something was terribly wrong, Alex soon realized, and opened her eyes, only to stare into the eyes of Brian from her class. Brian was, the most disgusting of all the boys, the one who never showered, always picked his nose in class, and smelled like cheese. Behind him, from behind the couch, up jumped three girls from their class. They stood right behind Brian, and so did Leonora. They were all laughing and pointing their fingers at Alex.

"DYKE!" Leonora yelled. "I knew you were a disgusting lesbian!"

"Dyke, dyke, dyke!"

All the girls laughed, while Leonora pulled out a tape recorder from under her pillow and pressed play.

"Yes, I want to kiss you," Alex heard her own voice say. Then Leonora rewound the tape, and played the bit over and over again. "Yes, I want to kiss you, Leonora. Yes, I want to kiss you, Leonora."

Alex stared at the girl she had loved so deeply, the girl she had adored beyond anything in this world, while Leonora laughed along with the other girls, mocking Alex, telling her how they had been playing her all this time, how Leonora was never her friend, that she would never belong anywhere, that they would play the tape at school to warn every girl about her, warn her that all she wanted was to get into their pants.

"No one will ever be your friend again, Alex," Leonora said. "No one."

That night, the boy held his sister in his arms, while she cried and swore she would kill all of them.

"I'll beat them to death," she said. "I'm gonna beat them all to death."

35

I GOT some expert to tell me that it was actually not an easy task in this country to get ahold of a real police-baton. Not the same type they used within the force. They were handed out only to officers, and just like their guns, they had to hand them back when they left the force.

"They have serial numbers, just like guns, so they know if one is missing," he stated.

"But, it could have been stolen, right?" I asked.

"Yes. But, again, the police would know if one was missing. Of course, no system is perfect, but in theory it shouldn't be happening."

I wrote it all down and put it in an article. I called the police station for a comment, but they didn't have one, they told me. Just as I had expected. No matter how this turned out, someone in the police had made a mistake. Either someone had lost his or her baton, or the killer was within the force. That made a pretty good article, I believed.

When I was done, I called Sune. I needed him to come down and take pictures for me, as I did the vox-pop. He sounded exhausted when he answered.

"You have a job," I said.

"Come on, Rebekka."

"Now what? I let you sleep in and you're still mad? I don't get you."

"Can't you get someone else to do it? I don't feel well."

I growled. I wanted to throw the phone at the wall. "That's because you're hung over. Maybe if you didn't go out drinking on a Thursday night with your friend, then this wouldn't happen."

"Yeah…well…" Sune said, sounding completely indifferent.

"You know what?" I said. "I'll find someone else. Someone who would like to work and make money. You just stay in bed."

I hung up before he could say anything. I was so angry I could explode. What the hell was he thinking? He was about to ruin everything for himself. If he started saying no to jobs, he was soon going to be out of work completely. I didn't understand what was going on with him. Could it be a late teenage rebellion after all? Who was he rebelling against? Me?

I grabbed the phone and pressed a number.

"Hey there," David said. "Good to hear from you."

"I have a job for you. I'm missing my photographer again. Don't ask. Could you step in? I know it's on short notice."

"No worries. I'm in the neighborhood anyway. I'll stop by the office. See you in a few minutes."

Working with David felt so good. We walked across town and ended up in the square, where we started interviewing people, asking them how they felt about the killings, if they were scared.

Of course, they all were terrified. Who wouldn't be? Four killings was certainly something to creep people out. Especially with the way they were killed. Beaten to death, then dressed up and displayed. And, yes, then there were the details about the cut off genitals. That was the most terrifying part, most people seemed to agree.

"If he did it while they were still alive, it must have hurt like crazy," an old lady carrying grocery bags said. Her eyes flamed with excitement as she spoke. I got the feeling she thought it was all very thrilling. Like a TV show or something.

"So, you're not afraid to go out?" I asked.

The old lady shivered. "Oh, yes, I am. I'm horrified, but you gotta eat, don't you? I don't have anybody to shop for me. And to think we can't even trust the police anymore. What is this world coming to?"

Another woman we interviewed told us she thought she knew who the killer was.

"He's my neighbor. I tell you. It's gotta be him. He's a policeman. I see him every day when he leaves the house in his uniform. He looks at me like he wants to beat me with that baton of his. I always knew he was up to no good."

"Now, there are a lot of police officers around town; they're not all killers, just because they suspect one of them to be," I argued.

"Oh, no. But it's him. I just know it is. You mark my words."

I shook my head and noted what she said. David took her picture, and we thanked her before approaching someone else. This time, it was a guy, around fifty. He looked shyly at us as we walked closer.

"Excuse me," I said. "We're from *Zeeland Times*. Would you mind answering some questions?"

"I don't know, maybe," the guy said.

"It's about the four killings. We're just trying to take the temperature of the population. How they're feeling about all this and so on."

The man stared at me strangely. "Well, I feel horrible. I can tell you that much," he said. "I knew one of the victims. Or, rather, I knew her daughter. Pastor Kemp's daughter Camilla. I went to school with her. I wasn't too fond of the mother, but the daughter was so nice. Beautiful as well. Such a shame."

"Why weren't you fond of the pastor? I thought she was very popular around here?" I asked.

"Well, not that it's important, but her daughter was homosexual, and the mother never approved of that. She threw her out and told her never to come back. Camilla died of AIDS back in the nineties and they never made up. Today, the mother still preaches against homosexuality. You'd think the death of her daughter would make her change her mind, huh? Well, now she's gone."

"She was against homosexuals?" I asked, when another piece of the puzzle suddenly fell into place. I looked at David.

"Yes, I even heard that she tried to help families with homosexual teenagers to convert their children, so to speak. You know how some people think it's a disease and that it can be cured. But I don't know if that's true."

36

"There's the connection," I said to David, as we walked back towards the office. "At least between the therapist and the pastor."

He nodded pensively. "But what about the others? The couple in the lake? Were they fighting against gay rights as well?"

"That's what we need to find out," I said, and sped up.

We walked into the office and I showed David to the computer where Sune usually sat. It looked strange to have someone else sitting there, especially David, since I knew how Sune felt about David. Sara thought it was exciting to have someone like David in our editorial room. She kept glancing at him and making small moaning sounds when he got up and walked to the restroom or to the kitchen to get coffee.

"He's so handsome," she whispered, as soon as he was out of the room.

David loaded the pictures and we started picking out the right ones for the vox-pop. David went to the bakery to get us sandwiches for lunch, while I wrote the article. As soon as it was sent and we had eaten, we both sat at my computer and started researching.

The couple from the lake had been identified as Dan and Tina Toft. They were a couple in their fifties. They used to live in a house in the middle of Karrebaeksminde. He was a lawyer; she was a secretary. Everything about them seemed very ordinary.

"According to this, they're leaving behind a son," David said.

I shrugged. "We should talk to him, then. What's his name?"

"Hans Toft."

"Can we find him?" I asked.

"I don't know. It's a pretty common name. But it's worth a try. Let me do just a simple search." David reached over and tapped on the keyboard. "There you go. There are forty-four with that name in Denmark. Apparently, none of them live around here. The closest is in Roervig, more than an hour and a half from here."

"But, it might as well be any of the other forty-three out there," I said with a sigh.

"You're right," he said, and picked up his cup and drank from it. Even when he sipped coffee he was attractive.

"I say we simply go to the couple's address and talk to the neighbors. What do you say?" I asked. "Maybe do a little vox-pop out there and ask them how they feel and so on. Maybe snoop around a little. According to the police report, they were killed in their home and then taken to the lake."

David put his cup down and smiled. "Sounds like a plan to me."

I grabbed my phone and looked at the display, hoping Sune would have called, or at least texted, but he hadn't. I sighed and put on my jacket. David looked at me with a smile.

"Are you alright?" he asked when we got outside.

"I guess," I said. "It's just Sune. It's strange. He hangs out with our neighbor constantly, and last night he came home drunk, and today he didn't even bother to show up when I called about this job. I don't know what to do about him."

We walked towards the car in silence, while I wondered what to do about Sune and our relationship. I missed him like crazy, and I hated myself for enjoying David's company this much. I felt so disloyal for discussing Sune behind his back, and especially with David. I couldn't stop wondering about that text David had sent me the night before, telling me he missed me. What did he mean by that? Did I want him to want more out of this than just friendship?

David put his hand on my shoulder. His touch warmed me. My stomach was hurting with sadness.

"It's okay, Rebekka. You can talk to me about anything. I'm your friend, remember?"

"I know," I said. "It's just so hard to explain. I mean, it's like I hardly know who he is anymore. It's like he's pulling away from me. The past few days have been a nightmare. I don't know what to do. It's like he'd rather I left him completely alone, but I'm afraid that if I do I'll lose him."

"Maybe it's just a phase," he said. "Maybe he needs to act out a little and have some space to figure things out. Then he'll come back to you."

"But I just...I get so angry at that Jeppe guy. Ever since he came into our lives, everything has changed. It changed Sune completely. I really hate him."

David tilted his head. "Do you really think it is fair to blame everything on him? Yes, he came into your lives and everything changed, Sune changed, but could it be that Sune might have acted out anyway? If it hadn't been this guy, maybe he would have...maybe found someone else to act out with?"

"You meant the problem goes deeper than that?" I asked.

"Yeah. Maybe it would make things easier if you simply accepted this Jeppe guy."

I pressed the remote and unlocked the car. "You really think so?"

"Plus, you can't really force him to do anything, you'll only end up pushing him further away. Give him the space he needs, and then he'll realize how great a life he has."

"So, what you're basically saying is…I have no choice. Accept the way things are and hope for the best? Doesn't sound very reassuring."

David opened the door to the passenger seat, then paused and smiled. "I wish I could say something else to make you feel better, but…"

"Well, that's not your fault."

I sat in the driver's seat, thinking about Sune and this Jeppe guy. Had the troubles started when he came into our lives, or were they already there? Was David right? I had put all my anger and frustration on Jeppe, thinking he was the problem, but maybe it had started long before this.

The thought didn't make me feel any better.

37

Leonora Christina Stroem shared a name with royalty, but that was about all she had in common with the princess that was the daughter of King Christian the 4th, back in the seventeenth century.

While the princess was engaged at only nine years old, and later married and had ten children, Leonora Christina had never met the right man, and never had any children, much to her regret. Well, at least not yet. At the age of almost twenty-nine, she wasn't out of the race just yet, even if her mother believed it was all over for her.

"He's never going to leave his wife. You must know that by now," she kept telling her.

But, Leonora believed he would. At least that's what he kept telling her he was going to do. And she believed him. Even after four years together, she believed he would soon tell his wife that it was over.

"I just need to wait till after the vacation to Bermuda," he had told her. "It would simply ruin the vacation if I told her before we went, and I can't do that to the children."

"Of course not."

"What was it he said the last time?" her mother now said on the phone, when Leonora explained to her what Morten had told her. It was Friday afternoon, and she had just come back from the firm when her mother had called. What a way to kick off the weekend.

"Oh, yes, he had to wait till after the wife's surgery," the mother continued.

"Well, he could hardly spring this on her right before she went into surgery," Leonora said. "You can't blame him for that. They have, after all, been married for fourteen years and have two children together. It's a big thing to split up after that much history together."

"It was plastic surgery, Leonora. Don't you see it?" her mother argued. "It's the same damn thing every time you ask him. He keeps coming up with excuses. It's been four years now! Don't you want a family? Don't you want to move on?"

She did. But the thing was, she really loved him. He was everything to her. They had met at the law firm. She was an associate and he was one of the partners. Morten had hired her four years ago, when she was fresh out of law school. She had been the youngest in the firm. On a conference trip to Aalborg, the northern part of Denmark, he had made a pass at her at the hotel bar. She had let him, since she had been intoxicated by him and the way he talked. They had sex in the hotel room all four nights they spent there, and while lying there, Morten had started complaining about his wife.

"I want out," he had said. "I can't stand her. But there's always the children, you know?"

It was his second time around, he had told her. He had a child with another woman that he was married to for only a few years, when he'd met his current wife, who he'd had an affair with until it was discovered.

"She got pregnant, and I had to marry her. It was a mistake. She was nothing but a fling, a flirt, and now I'm stuck with her. She's nothing like you. You smell incredible. You're so beautiful I can hardly believe it. I have never been with a woman this beautiful."

He had asked her to save herself for him, and she had liked that. Soon, he bought her an apartment close to the firm, where they would meet up during lunch breaks or in the afternoon when his wife thought he was working late. He would tell her how amazing she was, how deeply he loved her and wanted to be with her instead of his dreadful wife. So, Leonora had decided to wait for him, wait for him to find the right time to leave his wife. And she knew he would eventually, because he really couldn't stand her. But there was always something. Always something they had to wait for. Leonora was saddened every time he postponed it, but at the same time, she found it very appealing that he was so concerned about his wife and children's wellbeing that he didn't want them to be hurt. It would happen. It just had to be at the exact right time.

"But the right time will never come, Leonora," her mother hissed on the phone. Leonora was tired of having the same conversation over and over with her mother, and tried to end it.

"Listen, I got to…"

"You're stupid, Leonora. Such a waste…"

Leonora felt the tears build up in her eyes. She felt so exhausted. So tired of hoping and waiting. So tired of having to defend herself and him. It was, after all, her life, wasn't it?

"There's someone at the door," she lied. "Gotta go. Bye, Mom."

Tears rolled across Leonora's cheeks as she hung up the phone. In many ways, she didn't have anything in common with the famous princess from the seventeenth century, but she did have one thing in common besides the name. They both ended up living their life in a prison because of a man.

While wiping her eyes with a tissue, she was interrupted by the sound of someone actually knocking on the door. Thinking it might be him, Leonora corrected her shirt and make-up in the mirror before she went to open the door. She peeked through the peephole before she opened the door, and was disappointed to find it wasn't Morten stopping by after work.

It was just a police officer.

38

"What can I do for you, Officer?"

The man looked at the girl and smiled. He couldn't quite figure out how he was feeling, standing in front of her again… a mixture of sadness, excitement and fury. How he loathed her. She was still as beautiful as back then. He understood why Alex had loved her so deeply. But he also remembered how his sister had cried, devastated by what she had done to her. He could still hear her crying when going to sleep at night, thinking no one would ever be able to love her. Thinking she was incapable of making anyone love her.

Leonora shook her head. "Officer? Is everything alright?"

The man smiled. "Oh, yes, yes. Sorry about that. I'm just going around the neighborhood. We have had a series of robberies in this complex. Have you seen anything suspicious around here?"

Leonora shook her head with a sniffle. Had she been crying? She seemed sad, almost hurt. It pleased the man.

"No, Officer. I haven't. You say someone broke into our complex? Did they steal anything?"

"Yes, last night someone broke into the apartment above yours. The owners came home while he was still there, and he ran to the balcony and climbed down. We suspect he must have landed on your balcony before he jumped to the ground. Could I take a look?"

Leonora stepped aside. "Of course, Officer. I haven't seen anything. But that is very upsetting news. I mean, I was home all night last night and didn't hear anything."

The man walked inside the apartment and Leonora closed the door behind him. He smiled gently to make her feel comfortable in his presence.

"Have I seen you before?" she asked, while he followed her through the hallway. It was a huge apartment. Beautiful high ceilings with stucco. The floors, old and wooden, creaked as they walked across them.

"You might have seen me around," the man answered.

"Well, I see a lot of officers around in my line of work," she said.

They entered the living room. The man took a thorough look around. Just as he suspected. It was nicely decorated with expensive designer furniture. Everything was white and light.

"So, were you alone last night?" he asked.

Leonora paused. She looked like she was thinking about the answer. Then she shook her head. "No. Someone was here with me. But he left at nine."

"About the time when the burglary took place. I might need the name of this guy that visited."

"Of course, Officer," she said, sounding concerned. "The balcony is right out here." She pointed at the sliding glass doors. She had teak patio furniture. Everything was just so perfect.

"It's funny," she said. "I really feel like I know you from

somewhere. Did we go to school together? We're about the same age, I think."

The man shook his head. "I'm not from around here."

"That's so strange. I could have sworn...you look just like...those eyes...are you sure you didn't used to go to Karrebaek Elementary? No, maybe I'm just confusing you with someone else. It was such a long time ago."

"Fourteen years to be exact," the man said.

Leonora froze. "So, it is you? But..."

"I'm her brother," the man said. "Her twin brother."

Leonora snapped her fingers. "That's right. Alex had a twin brother. I had completely forgotten. I'm so sorry for what happened to her. It's so sad."

The man tilted his head, then smiled. He could tell it confused Leonora. A flinch of fear appeared in her eyes.

"Wait. Why did you say you weren't from around here just before?" she asked. "And why are you looking at me like that?"

The man grabbed his baton and pulled it out of his belt. The fear grew in Leonora's eyes.

"What is this?" Leonora asked. "What do you want from me? We were nothing but kids back then. You must know that. It was just a prank. We were just joking around with her..."

"Oh, it was just a joke, was it?"

"Y...yes."

"Really? 'Cause I could have sworn it almost killed my sister. I could have sworn it felt like she was falling and falling into a deep darkness she never escaped from again. But, maybe I was wrong? After all, it was just a JOKE!"

The man laughed out loud. Leonora jumped at the sound of his laughter.

"What's so funny? Why are you laughing?" she asked with a trembling voice.

"I just thought of another joke," he said, swinging the baton till it slammed into her face, breaking her nose and cracking her lip. Blood spurted into the man's face and onto his white teeth.

"You will simply loooove its *punch* line."

39

"They were the nicest couple. I was petrified when I heard what happened. I simply couldn't believe it. And now they say it might be a police officer who did this awful thing to them?"

The woman living next door to the Toft couple had invited us inside of her house and served us coffee and cookies.

"Did you know them well?" I asked, while David took a couple of pictures of her as she spoke.

"As well as neighbors do around here, I guess," she said with a sigh. "I mean, we spoke mostly in the summer when we could spend time in the yard and talk over the hedge, but other than that, we didn't associate much. They kept mostly to themselves."

"How long did they live in the house next door?" I asked.

"Oh, they've been here for many years. I don't know exactly how long. I bought this house only three years ago."

"Have you ever met the son?" David asked, while looking at her through the lens. I could tell he was used to doing this kind of thing on his own.

She looked up at him, and he shot a series of photos.

"I didn't even know they had a son," she said. "I mean, the

other neighbors told me they had one, but I never saw him myself. I don't think he came around much, and they never spoke of him. Some say they used to have two children. Twins, they say, but I don't know if it's true or not. They say something happened to one of them." The woman gestured with a sigh. "I'm sorry I can't be of more help. Maybe if you ask Mr. Severinsen on the other side of the street. He might know more. He has been here longer."

"We might try that," I said, and got up. I signaled David to wrap it up. We had enough for the article, and she didn't seem to know much else.

We thanked her for her help and the coffee and went across the street and rang the doorbell.

Mr. Severinsen opened the door. He was an elderly man who looked to be about the same age as my dad.

"Yes?"

"Hello, my name is Rebekka Franck, this is David Busck, we work for *Zeeland Times* and we're doing a story about Dan and Tina Toft who lived across the street from you."

"They're dead," he grumbled. "Nothing more to tell."

"Well, we believe there is. I mean, they were killed, brutally murdered in their own home. How do you think that has affected the neighborhood?"

"I ain't afraid," Mr. Severinsen said.

"So, what happened to them doesn't scare you?" I asked.

"That's what I said, isn't it?"

"Yes, it was." I noted it on the pad, and then looked up at the old man. "How well did you know them?"

"Hardly ever spoke with them. Nice couple, though. Kept their driveway clean and cut the hedge on time every summer. Nothing much to complain about. Not like all those newcomers around here."

"So, you know their son?" I asked.

"I won't say I know him."

"But you lived here when he still lived at home?" I asked.

"Yes. They were the strangest kids I have ever met. Something was really off about the girl. You could tell by the way she comported herself. It was just wrong."

"So, there were two kids? Were they twins?"

"Couldn't tell them apart until they let the girl's hair grow long and put dresses on her. Poor kid. All she wanted was to be like her brother. All she wanted was to play ball and ride her bike like the boys. But the parents wouldn't have it. They had her put on those pretty dresses and play with dolls. She wanted to wear pants and play with the boys. I never understood what was so wrong about that? When she became a teenager, she looked terrible. She was only allowed to wear dresses, but to rebel against her parents, all she wore were black dresses, and with her all black hair, she came off a little freakish, like those Satan worshippers or Goth or what they call themselves. And then, the way she moved. It was awkward. She was so masculine. Not feminine and petite like the other girls. She was big for her age. Both in height and size. The kids here on the street were cruel to her. Called her monster or giant. But, when she got older, like fourteen-fifteen, she was so much stronger than the others. She would beat the crap out of them. They still called her names, though. She was probably best known around here as *the lesbo*. Kids can be so cruel. I mean, so what if she liked girls? But, worst of all, was that the parents never accepted her. Anyway, that's all I know."

"So, you don't know where they are today?"

"No. I have no idea."

"Thank you so much for all your help," I said, and was about to leave when the old man stopped us.

"Wait a minute. I have something."

He disappeared for a second, then came back with an old photo. "I want you to give this to them if you ever find them. I tried to look them up to send it, but couldn't locate them anywhere. I'm getting old. The wife died last year, and I don't know how long I have myself. I don't want it to get lost when I die. The twins might like to have it."

I nodded and grabbed the picture. I looked at it. It showed a family of four standing in front of their house. The children were twins. A girl and a boy. Both had thick black hair. The girl's face was almost covered by her long hair, like she was trying to hide from the world.

"It was taken when the twins were about eight or nine. I took it with my camera at a block party in '94. The only one we ever had around here. Anyway, if you could make sure one of them gets it, I would be very pleased."

"We'll do our best," I said.

"Thank you. Have a nice day."

Mr. Severinsen closed the door, and we started walking back to the car parked in front of Tina and Dan Toft's house. I realized we had parked right in the spot where the photograph had been taken twenty-one years ago. I couldn't believe the story I had just heard. In the picture, they seemed like an ordinary happy family. The parents hadn't wanted to accept her for who she was. Had she returned and killed them because of that?

"So, at least there seems to be some sort of silver lining here," David said, while shooting a few pictures of the house that had once contained an entire family with all their expectations for the future.

"You're thinking about the homosexual theme?" I asked.

"Yeah. The daughter was apparently a lesbian. The parents didn't want to accept her the way she was."

"Like the pastor and the therapist. There is definitely a theme here. But, I can't wrap my mind around the motive."

We got back inside the car and I started it, when my phone suddenly rang. It was Sara.

40

"Something is going on at an address downtown," she said, sounding agitated.

I looked at my watch. I had to pick up the kids in less than an hour, or I would be late.

"Are you sure it's important?" I asked.

"Positive. They've called for help from Copenhagen," Sara continued. "The blue vans are on their way. You know what that means."

"Crime scene technicians," I said, and looked at David, while wondering what to do with the kids. Could I get ahold of Sune? Could I trust him to pick them up and not forget about it? I had to.

"Text me the address and we're on it," I said, and hung up.

"Another job?" David asked.

"Yeah. I'm gonna have to ask you to stick around for a little while longer. Can you do that?"

"I don't have anything better to do," he said.

I found Sune's number in my phone and called him.

"Come on, pick up," I mumbled.

Luckily, Sune picked up right away. He sounded like he was still sleeping. "What's up?" he asked.

What's up? What is he? Sixteen?

"I need you to pick up the kids today. Something's going on downtown, and I have to go and check it out."

Sune sighed. "You are, or you and David are?" he asked.

"Hey," I snarled, a little more angrily than intended. He just annoyed me so much right now. "That's your own fault. You were the one who opted out when I called you. If you had said yes earlier, you would have been the one going on this job now."

"I wasn't feeling well. I'm much better now," he said. "I could be there in ten minutes if I took the bike."

"You know it doesn't work like that. The newspaper already hired David for the entire day. We can't pay for two photographers. You know how it is. Besides, I really need you to pick up the kids today. Can you do that for me?"

Sune sighed. "I don't have a car."

"You can walk. It's not very far. Take the stroller for William and have Julie and Tobias walk. It won't hurt any of you to get a little exercise. Hopefully, I'll be home within a couple of hours."

Sune paused for a long time. "Okay," he said. "I'll take care of it."

"Thank you!" I smiled and held the phone close to my ear. I hated this strange thing that had come between us lately. I felt so far away from him. I wanted to tell him I loved him, that I missed him so much, but somehow the words didn't leave my lips.

"See you at home," he said.

"Yes, see you," I said and hung up.

I looked at David, who tilted his head. He looked worried.

"Is everything alright? I don't want to come in between the two of you, Rebekka. I enjoy this immensely. I love hanging out with you, and working again makes me feel great, but if it causes any problems between you and Sune, then I'm gone. You just say the word."

I sighed.

"No. It's not your fault. Besides, one of us needs to pick up the kids anyway."

"So, it's alright?"

Part of me wanted to say no. Part of me wanted to talk to David and tell him how my stomach was one big knot with worry about Sune and me, but there wasn't time, and the rest of me didn't want to involve him any more than he already was. It always made me feel like I was betraying Sune. So, instead of telling him how badly it hurt that I was suddenly unable to talk to my boyfriend, the father of my child, I smiled and swallowed my emotions.

"Yes. Sune's picking up the kids, and we're good to go."

41

Losing Leonora in her life was bad for Alex. As a grown man, later in life, he couldn't escape the feeling of despair that his sister had gone through in the months after the incident in Leonora's bedroom. People laughed at Alex in school. It was worse than ever.

The man thought about how much he hated seeing her like this, as he watched another officer set up the red and white tape to block the entrance of Leonora's building. A crowd had gathered outside, where the police cars had parked in the street, and people around him were talking amongst themselves, wondering what was going on. The man told them to stay back. Above them, the sky had turned grey, and he was expecting it to rain sometime soon. That would clear the streets.

He watched the doctor arrive to declare her dead, and thought with pleasure of the look in her eyes when she had realized what was about to happen. He had dreamt for many years of revenging his sister for what Leonora and those other kids had done to her.

I'm a freak! I don't want to live anymore!

The screaming at night was back, and now Alex was cutting herself with razorblades. She hardly ate anything and became so skinny the doctors had to force-feed her with a tube. As her brother, he knew how bad it was, and how much she just wanted to disappear, to vanish. He was terrified of one day waking up and realizing she wasn't there anymore.

She got herself into a lot of trouble at school. In anger, she would attack other students and beat them senseless. And being bigger than most of them, she succeeded in terrifying many of them. It didn't stop the mocking and name-calling, but now they only did it behind her back and not to her face anymore. She hung out with her brother at school, but he knew she really just wanted to be with Leonora, that she longed to be with her again.

When they turned sixteen, it started to affect her mental health. Their parents relied on Dr. Korner and Dr. Winter, and the visits to their offices became more and more frequent. But Alex was slipping. It became obvious that she had a hard time staying in reality. She was losing touch, and more and more often she lived in a fantasy world of her own, where she was allowed to be anything she wished. Where she could be the boy she had always believed she was.

Still, the doctors fought to keep her in reality, in the real world, and kept telling her she was a girl, and soon they started medicating her. She was diagnosed with schizophrenia, and the doctors told their parents that maybe that had been the issue all along. She was depressed, suffered from anxiety attacks, and it was the cause for her growing isolation, they believed. She was suicidal and needed to be under observation.

Six months after the incident in Leonora's bedroom, Alex was admitted to a mental institution called Nordvang, where she stayed for six weeks under Dr. Winter's supervision. When she came back, her brother hardly recognized her. She wouldn't talk to him, and if he approached her, she would hiss like a cat and pretend to want to scratch him with her nails. It troubled him deeply, and he felt like he had lost her. She was doped up on medication, and seemed to have slipped even further into a world of her own.

He started to fear her slightly, and stayed out of her way. Their parents hid anything she could use to cut herself: knives, scissors, and razorblades. At night, she would scream even louder than before, and this time not because she was sad, but she screamed like a crazy person. One night, when she screamed like that, her brother crawled up to her in her bed like he always did when she cried at night. Only this time, he wasn't welcome any longer. Alex was sitting up in the bed, her hair hanging down in front of her face. She was holding a pair of scissors in her hand, using them to cut into her fingers. Blood was dripping on the sheets.

"What are you doing?" he asked, terrified. "You're not allowed to have these. How did you get those scissors? Give them to me. You're hurting yourself."

But Alex didn't hand them over. She looked at her brother through the long hair with contempt, her piercing blue eyes cutting through his bones. Then, she lifted the scissors in the air and pierced them through his right hand, nailing it to the rail.

42

It was late before I made it home. I had dropped David off at his hotel and thanked him for all his help. After getting all the pictures we could, standing under an umbrella in the rain, and talking to Officer Pedersen, who was on the scene as usual, we went back to the office and I had written the story about the young lawyer who had been found killed in her own apartment. The police still wouldn't tell me if it had anything to do with the other four recent killings in our small town, but I had a feeling it did. Officer Henrik Pedersen had told me, without getting into details, that it was ugly. We had waited for hours in the darkness outside the apartment complex to see the body being taken away, and even though it was covered up on the stretcher, an arm fell down, and I could tell she was wearing a suit with cufflinks. Being a lawyer, it wasn't that odd, but I had a feeling this wasn't what she had been wearing at the office. I didn't mention anything in the article, since it was all guessing, but I was determined to find out the very next day.

With Sune's help.

I yawned and parked the car in the driveway, then looked

at my watch. It was almost midnight. I hadn't been home this late in many months. I just hoped everything had been all right with the kids. I couldn't wait to spend a calm weekend with my family. Hopefully, the killer would take a break as well.

As I came closer to the house, I could hear voices coming from inside. Agitated voices, and I wondered what was going on. I could suddenly hear children's voices, yelling and screaming loudly.

Are the children still up?

I grabbed the door handle and swung the door open. The yelling got louder, and I hurried to the living room, where I found all of them in front of the big screen TV playing X-box. Julie, Tobias, Sune, Jeppe, and...*William?*

I stared, baffled, at all of them. Julie saw me and ran towards me. She was literally paler than the white shirt she was wearing.

"Mom! You're home." She walked over empty pizza boxes, hugged me, and Sune paused the game.

"Hi, Rebekka," he said.

William was sitting on the floor, playing with his blocks, looking like he was on speed...with his eyes wide open and smiling.

Sune approached me and kissed me. I stared at him, not knowing what to say to not sound like his mother.

"Do you have any idea what time it is?" I asked.

Sune shrugged. "Yeah, I know it's kind of late. But it's Friday, and we were having so much fun. We can sleep in tomorrow."

"Sleep in? Are you kidding me? William is not even two years old and you expect him to sleep in? He can't stay up till midnight!"

Sune took a step backwards. "Whoa. Have you looked at

him? He's having the time of his life. Need I remind you that he is my son too, and I say he is doing just fine?"

My hands were shaking in anger, and I had nowhere to put it. How could he be so irresponsible? I mean, I knew Sune was just a kid, and that every now and then, he did things in ways I never would, but this was over the top. This was simply too much for me to bear. I stared at Jeppe, who started the game again.

"Could you maybe tell your friend that the party is over and that he has to leave?" I asked Sune. "We have a child that wakes up at six in the morning, and tomorrow he is going to be a pain in the neck because he's so tired."

Jeppe put the console down and put his hands in the air. "I'm sorry," he said. "I'll leave right away." He smiled and approached me. "I really am sorry, Rebekka, if I caused any trouble. I guess time just slipped. We were having a lot of fun. I didn't mean to...I mean, I just enjoy their company so much. I feel alone every now and then. You have such a beautiful family."

It was so strange, looking at this guy that resembled Sune so much with the Mohawk and spiked leather band. He smiled gently, and I couldn't stay mad at him. This wasn't his fault, after all. It was Sune who was the father; he was supposed to be the responsible one. Jeppe hadn't done anything wrong, for all I knew.

"It's okay," I said. "It's just been a long day, that's all."

"I'll leave you to get some sleep then," Jeppe said, and grabbed his jacket from the back of my dad's favorite recliner.

"Thanks for helping me today," Sune yelled after him. Jeppe waved and then left.

Sune looked angry at me. "Why do you have to embarrass me like this every time I spend time with Jeppe?"

Was he kidding me?

"Embarrass you?" I asked, sensing I was about to explode.

"How about how you're treating me? I asked you to pick up the children..."

"And I did. I picked them up, walked all the way down there, even though it started to rain on our way back. Luckily, Jeppe was able to pick us up and get us home. Otherwise, we'd been soaking wet. I do everything you tell me to, just not always the way you want it done. You are so controlling, and want everyone to do everything the way you think it's supposed to be done. But I got news for you. It doesn't have to be like that. Sometimes, a good father is someone who plays with his kids, and not someone who does everything by the book of Rebekka!"

"You know what?" I said.

Julie cleared her throat. I turned to look at her. I had completely forgotten that they were still in the room. She pointed at William, who had fallen asleep on top of his blocks.

"He passed out," she said. "Do you want me to take him up to his room and tuck him in?"

I was overwhelmed with guilt. "I'm sorry," I said, and grabbed William from the floor. Tobias stared at me with tears in his eyes. Julie followed my every move closely.

"Are you guys breaking up?" she asked.

The question surprised me. I shook my head, then grabbed her and hugged her tightly.

"No, sweetie. We're just having an argument. Just like you and Tobias sometimes argue, right Sune?"

I turned to look at him. He smiled and approached the children. I signaled to Tobias to come closer, and then hugged him as well. Sune put his long arms around all of us.

"We're a family now," he said. "Families disagree, but they stick together through it."

I smiled and leaned over and kissed Sune to show the children we still loved each other. The kiss felt forced, but that didn't matter. I kissed Julie, then Tobias on their cheeks.

"We'll be fine, okay guys? Takes more than a small argument to tear us apart," I said. "Now, it's time for bed, you two. It's way past your bedtime."

"Let me tuck them in," Sune said, and took William out of my hands. "Don't worry. I got it. You open a bottle of wine. It is, after all, Friday."

43

It had been a while since we had enjoyed each other's company as much as we did that night. Sune and I stayed up till two o'clock and talked and drank red wine like we used to do on Friday nights. We even snuck out at one point and smoked a cigarette on the patio like two teenagers.

"I missed this," I said, sitting on his lap in my dad's patio swing.

Sune grabbed the cigarette out of my hand and smoked it. "Me too," he said. "I miss being us and doing silly stuff together. Life can get too serious sometimes, you know?"

I nodded pensively. He was right. I had become too tense and too hung up on doing things properly. There was no room for just playing and doing things differently. After all, it was hardly going to harm any of the kids that they had stayed up late. It would likely do more harm for them to see us fight like that and to see their mother get angry. Maybe I had overreacted after all. Maybe I had been slightly jealous. They had just been hanging out having fun, while I had to work. And on top of it, I was on a case that was so creepy. It was so sad about what had happened to that girl.

"So, I've been thinking," Sune said, and handed me back the cigarette.

I smoked. "Yeah? About what?"

"About us. I think it's time we get our own place."

I froze. Not again? I hated when he brought that up. "I have to think about my father," I said.

"I know," Sune said. "But we have to think about ourselves as well. It's bothering me, having to live in your dad's house, constantly feeling like I have to be grateful to him, like I can't take care of my own family. It's getting to me."

I looked into Sune's eyes. I could tell he was being very serious. I couldn't blame him for wanting this. It made sense that it was bothering him. On top of everything, he was hardly making any money these days, since he hadn't had that many assignments for other magazines, and what he made off of *Zeeland Times* was hardly enough. It hurt his pride that I, on top of being the oldest, also supported the family, and we all lived in my dad's house. I caressed his cheek gently.

"I'm sorry, babe. I haven't been attentive enough to your needs," I said. "I think I get it. You want to be the man of the house."

Sune grabbed the cigarette from my fingers again. He smiled and nodded. "Something like that. Not quite as old-fashioned as you make it sound, but I guess that is it. I want us to be like a real family."

I shrugged. "I guess we could afford it."

Sune offered me the rest of the cigarette, but I shook my head. I didn't want anymore. He smiled and killed it under his shoe.

"Well, I guess that's it," he said. "The decision is made."

I felt a huge knot in my stomach, thinking about my dad. It would absolutely kill him to not have us around. Maybe if we found something really close by? It was time. Sune was right about that. I just wasn't sure I was ready.

Sune grabbed my face and pulled me close, then kissed me gently. I closed my eyes and enjoyed it. This time, it didn't feel forced at all. This time, we were both into it. He grabbed me and lifted me up, then carried me towards the door. I felt so small in his arms. I could tell he enjoyed taking charge.

Sune carried me all the way to our bedroom upstairs. He threw me on the bed. He pulled off my pants, then kissed the inner side of my thighs. I closed my eyes and enjoyed his touches. We hadn't been intimate like this for months, not since before the incident in the mines. I simply hadn't been well enough for it, and Sune had known to give me the time and space I needed. But now, it felt good. It felt right. We made love like we had just met, and somehow, in the darkness, we found each other again. At least for a little while.

We fell asleep afterwards, and about an hour later I woke up. Exactly what woke me up, I don't know, but I opened my eyes and realized someone was in our bedroom. I gasped and stared at the man in front of me.

When my eyes met his, he turned around and rushed out of the bedroom.

Then I screamed.

44

"What's going on!?"

Sune jumped up from his pillow.

"What's happening, Rebekka? Why are you screaming?"

"It was him. He was here...He was watching us in our sleep, Sune."

"What are you talking about? Who was?" Sune asked.

"Him! Jeppe! He was here. In our bedroom."

Sune shook his head. "What the heck are you talking about? There's no one here?"

"He ran out the door. He might still be in the house. How did he get in the house, Sune?"

Sune grabbed me by the shoulders and looked me in the eyes. "There's no one here. There never was. You were just dreaming."

I shook my head in frustration. "No, Sune. He was there. I saw him. He was standing right over there by the door. And he was looking at us. It scared the crap out of me. What if he is still in the house?"

"Okay. Okay. I'll go check and see if anyone is here, if that will make you feel better. I still believe it was just a very vivid dream," he said, while putting on his pants.

Sune left and I walked to the door to listen in if something happened to him. I knew Tobias had a baseball bat in his room in case I needed it. Sune stumbled around downstairs before he came back up again.

"Like I said, there's no one there."

"Did you check the front door? Was it locked?" I asked.

Was it just a dream? No, he was there. I saw him. I did. I know I did.

"Yes, it was locked. So was the back door. No windows were open. No one could have come in here. Now, can we please just go back to sleep?"

"He was here, Sune. I'm not making it up. I swear. He was standing right in the corner. The door was open. It was him, Sune. It really was."

I could tell he didn't believe me. He shook his head and we walked back into the bedroom. "It was a dream, Rebekka. I'm sure it felt very real in the moment, but it wasn't. Trust me. Why would Jeppe come into our bedroom and look at us? Give me one reason?"

"Because he's creepy?" I said.

Sune laughed. "You think Jeppe is creepy?"

"A little. I mean, the whole look-alike thing is kind of creepy."

Sune put his arm around my shoulder and laughed again. "You've been working on too many murder cases, my dear. Jeppe is just a nice guy, trying hard to be our friend. That's all. Now, can we get some sleep? I'm beat."

We went back to bed, but it took a long time before I finally fell asleep. I kept looking at the door and wondering if he would come back. I still wasn't convinced that it was just a dream. How could it be? He was there.

Finally, I gave in and dozed off. A few hours later, I woke

to the sound of William crying. I rushed into his room and picked him up. He needed a clean diaper. I changed him, then walked downstairs to make him breakfast. It was still dark outside at six o'clock, and I felt like I was the only one awake in the entire nation.

After his breakfast, I took William to the living room, where he played with blocks for an hour or so, while I dozed off on the couch. Then, Julie and Tobias woke up and came downstairs. My dad followed them, holding onto his cane.

"I'll fix you all some breakfast," I said, and got up from the couch.

"You look awful," Julie said, as I put bread in the toaster.

My dad nodded. "Yes, you do look terrible, Rebekka. Have you slept at all?"

"Well, not much, I have to admit." The toast popped up, and I buttered it.

My dad looked at Julie and Tobias. "What do you say we give your mom some sleep, huh? We can take care of William for a few hours, can't we?"

"Yup," Julie said.

Tobias nodded.

My dad chuckled. "Go, dear. Go get your beauty sleep."

Needless to say, he didn't have to say that twice.

45

THE WEEKEND ENDED up being good for all of us. We spend both Saturday and Sunday in the comfort of our living room, playing board games and even the X-box. I finally gave in and let the kids show me how to play. To my surprise, I ended up liking it. Jens-Ole was happy with my articles in Saturday's paper, and didn't even call me once during the entire weekend.

I couldn't quite shake the experience of seeing Jeppe in our bedroom, but decided it wasn't something I wanted to argue with Sune about. I decided he was right, and to let it go. It had to have been a dream. Anything else would be too strange. And, yes, Jeppe was a little odd, but not that odd.

On Sunday afternoon, Sune asked me if it would be all right if he invited Jeppe over to play with us. At first, I wasn't sure I liked the idea, mainly because I really enjoyed being just us, but then I gave in. Jeppe came over and he and Sune watched a soccer game, while the kids and I played Monopoly. My dad had been with us most of the day, but now he decided to go back to bed.

I stared at Jeppe, while he and Sune chatted amicably and

drank their beers. They talked about soccer and players, and all that stuff that didn't interest me one bit. I tried to imagine him standing in our bedroom staring at me, but it somehow felt wrong now. It couldn't have been real, could it? He didn't seem so creepy, now that I was looking at him. He seemed so sweet all of a sudden. Plus, he made Sune happy. I had to learn to accept him as a part of his life.

"It's your turn, Mom," Julie said.

I grabbed the dice and threw it, when I heard William cry. I got up. "William is awake from his nap," I said. "I have to go and get him."

I walked up the stairs and into William's bedroom. He was standing up in his bed and crying. I grabbed him in my arms and hugged him, then took him to the changing table and put him down.

"Now there...no more need to cry. Let's get this dirty diaper off, shall we?"

I looked at my son and wondered when he was going to speak. He made sounds like he was trying to, but no real words yet. At this age, Julie had spoken like a waterfall. Mostly stuff only I understood, but she wouldn't shut up. Whereas, William could be quiet for hours. I had wondered if something was wrong, but the doctor had told me William probably was a late bloomer.

"And boys do tend to be a little slower than girls. That's just the way it is," he had said.

"You'll start talking to me soon, won't you?" I said, and tickled his tummy, when I suddenly sensed that someone was behind me. I turned to look into Jeppe's eyes. Everything inside of me froze.

Is he following me?

He smiled. "I'm sorry. I was looking for the bathroom."

The bathroom. He just took the wrong door. Got to stop being so paranoid, Rebekka.

"It's across the hallway," I said, and continued to look at my son.

"Oh, thank you," Jeppe said.

I put William's clean diaper on, then put a pair of clean pants on, and had him stand up while holding him.

"Oh, you're a big boy, now, huh?"

William laughed and grabbed my hair. I kissed him and took him in my arms. When I turned, Jeppe was still there, but he had moved even closer.

I gasped.

"Oh, my God. You startled me," I said, my heart beating like a drum.

What is he still doing here? Why hasn't he gone to the restroom?

I felt uncomfortable with him so close to me, and I tried to walk past him, but he blocked my way. Then he leaned over and whispered in my ear.

"I like that shirt, Rebekka. Red is my favorite color."

46

"That was you? You sent me those texts?"

I felt my face turn red in anger. Who the hell did he think he was?

Jeppe smirked.

"Answer me!" I yelled. "Did you send me those texts?"

He still didn't answer. The way he stared at me freaked me out. "It was you, wasn't it? And what about yesterday? I saw you in our bedroom. It was you, wasn't it? You were watching us. You were staring at us in our sleep, weren't you? You creep!"

Steps on the stairs came closer. Sune came inside William's bedroom. "What's going on here?"

Jeppe shrugged. "I don't know. I tell you, man. That girlfriend of yours is nuts. She suddenly attacked me with all these questions. She's apparently accusing me of staring at you in your sleep?"

"That again, Rebekka? Really? I thought we agreed it was just a dream."

I looked at Jeppe. I couldn't believe him. "I want you out of my house," I said. "I want you out of here now. You hear me?

And don't you dare to ever come back here. I don't want you near me or my children again."

"Rebekka!?" Sune said.

Jeppe turned to him. "It's okay, bro. I told you she was jealous of us. It's all right. I'll back out. I'll leave. No hard feelings. I'll see you around."

"No, you won't," I said, but he had already left.

Sune looked angrily at me. "What the hell are you doing, Rebekka? I didn't think you'd stoop this low. You really hit rock bottom with this. I can't believe you. I finally have a friend. I finally have someone I like to hang out with, and then you do this to me? I'm beginning to think he is right. You are jealous. You have been jealous of him and me this whole time. Just because you don't have any friends. What else is he right about, huh? He keeps telling me I should keep a closer eye on you and that David guy. You're probably cheating on me. Are you, Rebekka? Are you cheating on me?"

I shook my head. "Sune…Would you please listen to me?"

"No. No. I'm done listening to you. I'm done hearing you say all this crap about Jeppe and talking to me like I'm a baby."

"Sune, would you just listen?…I…"

Sune shook his head in anger. "No. I'm done here, Rebekka. We're done here. I'm gonna stay at Jeppe's tonight, and tomorrow I'll start looking for a new place for me and Tobias."

On the last word, Sune turned around before I could say anything, and stormed down the stairs.

"Sune!" I yelled, trying to run after him, but it was too late. When I reached the stairs, I heard the front door slam.

Tobias and Julie came out from the living room and looked at me. "What happened?" Julie asked. "First Jeppe left, now Sune?"

"Yeah," Tobias said. "Where did my dad go?"

I swallowed my emotions and forced a smile. "They just

went out for a little bit. They'll be back later. No worries, kids."

Of course, my daughter didn't buy that. She always saw right through me. "You look sad, Mommy. Did something happen? Did you and Sune fight again?"

I held on to William and hugged him tight, while fighting the tears. I sniffled and wiped my nose. "It's nothing. I'm fine," I said, my voice cracking. "Go ahead and finish the game without me. I'll be down a little later."

47

Monday morning came, and I still hadn't heard anything from Sune. I knew he was staying with Jeppe next door, but wanted to give him the space to think, so I didn't even try and call him. Even though it was devastating, since he clearly didn't want to listen to anything I had to say, and I wasn't very comfortable with him spending time with that creep. What was his agenda anyway? What did he want from us? Why was he spying on us at night? Why was he texting me? Did he have a thing for me? Or was he trying to split us up?

I drove the kids to school and headed off to work, while trying not to worry about Sune and our future. He had to come around somehow, and then I would be able to explain everything to him.

"Whoa. Someone either partied all weekend or the kids kept you up all night? Did William get sick or something?" Sara asked, when she saw me.

I sighed and sat at my desk. I was exhausted. Emotionally, completely shattered.

"Let me get you some coffee," Sara said, and disappeared

into the kitchen. She came back with a steaming hot cup. The best sight I had seen all morning.

"You're a doll, thank you so much," I said.

"With milk, just the way you like it," she chirped. How she was always in such a good mood on Monday mornings was beyond my comprehension. Even on the good days, I wasn't as cheerful as her. A plate with a pastry landed next to the coffee. Our eyes met, and Sara winked.

"You deserve it," she said. "I put a little honey in your coffee to sweeten you up a little," she whispered, then tiptoed back to her desk with a giggle.

She made me smile. The way she loved taking care of me was wonderful. The morning had been rough, having to take care of all three kids on my own, so I guess I did deserve it. And I had no time to get breakfast, so I was actually pretty hungry.

I grabbed the pastry and started eating. It was crisp on the outside and moist on the inside, just the way freshly baked pastry was supposed to be. A little jelly inside of it made it just perfect. I closed my eyes and enjoyed it, along with the sweet coffee. The combination of sugar and caffeine soon sparked life into me, and I felt more alive. I was ready for whatever this day had in store for me. I turned on my computer and a picture of Sune, the kids, and I screamed at me, and the knot in my stomach returned. Were we going to get through this? Did Julie have to go through yet another bad break-up? Why was I so terrible at relationships? Was Sune right? Was I too controlling?

"So, David called and said he was going to stop by this morning," Sara said. "He told me to let you know. He didn't want to call you on your cell, he said. Probably afraid of what Sune might think, huh? Does Sune have reason to be jealous, I wonder?"

I shook my head and sipped some more coffee. "I think I'm done with men for a little while," I said.

"So, you and Sune...?"

I shrugged. "I don't know what's going to happen. He didn't come home last night. It's a long story."

Sara looked terrified. "Don't tell me you're splitting up?"

I wanted to be honest with Sara, but also knew she adored Sune and me, and it would almost be as hard on her as on the kids if we split up.

"No. No," I said, sounding exactly like I had when trying to convince the kids that everything would be fine. "Just a little trouble, that's all. Nothing we can't fix. We just need a little time. You know how it is."

Sara hardly breathed. She had a hand on her chest and gasped as she spoke. "You're not...you and that David fellow, you're not...are you?"

"No. No. Not at all. We're just friends, that's all."

Sara breathed again. "Phew. 'Cause, I mean, the guy is handsome and all...but still. You and Sune. That's special."

My phone rang and I picked it up, happy to escape this conversation. It was Jens-Ole.

"I want you to follow up on that lawyer story, that girl that was killed. I was thinking you could go to the law firm and speak with her co-workers. Paint a picture of this girl. Who was she? Was she liked? Was she kinky and got herself into trouble? What's her story? Did Sune manage to find the autopsy report yet?"

"Sune? Well...No...He's..." I looked at Sara, who was signaling me, putting a hand to her forehead and pretending to lie down. "Sick. He's sick. Yes. Sune hasn't been well."

"I hope it's nothing serious?" Jens-Ole asked.

"No. Just the flu. You know how these things take a few days...sometimes a week. He'll do it as soon as he's better."

"Well, good. Tell him to feel better, and then bring that David guy. He's quite the photographer. I mean, for a journalist." Jens-Ole chuckled. "No, we've been very impressed with his work. He's a great replacement for Sune."

48

DAVID ARRIVED while I was thinking about my editor's bad choice of words.

Replacement. As if anyone could ever replace Sune.

"Everything all right?" he asked, with his handsome smile.

"It's a long story. I got a job for you. Jens-Ole wants us to go and talk to her colleagues in the law firm and paint a picture of her. We don't have much on her the way it is, and it is fairly rare that an associate in a prestigious law firm is found murdered."

"Sure," he said. "I wasn't doing much today anyway."

I looked at David, and wondered for a second why he was still here anyway? Why was he sticking around? He didn't have a job here. He didn't have any family here, to my knowledge. Was he just here for me? Because he thought I could somehow make him feel better? Because he enjoyed my company?

Maybe it was as simple as that.

Or maybe because he's madly in love with you and is just waiting for you to split up with Sune to make his move.

"You coming?" he asked.

I smiled and grabbed my jacket. "Sure. Let's do this."

There was another thought that occurred to me while we walked to my car. The killings had started just as David arrived in town.

Don't be an idiot, Rebekka. You know the guy. He saved you and took care of everyone else down in the sinkhole. He's a freaking hero.

No, it was stupid. There was nothing linking him to any of them, as far as I knew. I shook the thought and we drove to the law firm.

"So, any news on finding the twins?" David asked on the way.

"I haven't had the time to look into it myself," I said. "But I asked Sara to try and locate them, starting with Hans Toft. She has contacts in the strangest of places. She's good at stuff like that."

We arrived at the building where the law firm had their offices. It was an old beautiful white villa in a residential neighborhood just outside of Karrebaeksminde. Inside, it had wooden floors all over, high ceilings, and big windows overlooking a lake. I recognized the lake as being the same that one Steffen and his dog had found the bodies in. It was a huge lake, and his grandparents lived on a farm on the other side of it. I stared at the frozen landscape outside the big windows. Could it be a coincidence that the bodies turned up next to the law firm?

A secretary approached us. "What can I do for you?"

"We're from *Zeeland Times*. I'm Rebekka Franck, this is David Busck. We called earlier?"

"Yes. Mr. Kragh will be with you in a minute. Please take a seat."

We did, and soon after, a good looking man in his mid-forties came out of his office and approached us. His shoes clacked as he walked across the parquet. He was wearing an expensive suit and had thick black hair.

"Hello," he said, and we shook hands. He stared at me very intensely, undressing me with his eyes. It was very uncomfortable. "Let's go into my office and talk."

"So, you want to know about Leonora, huh?" he said, when we had sat down inside his office. He was still smiling and staring at me. I didn't smile back and avoided his eyes.

"Yes. We really don't have much information about her, but would like to do a portrait of a sort. Maybe you could help?"

Mr. Kragh leaned back in his leather chair behind the big desk. "Sure. If you think I can contribute anything, then by all means. What do you want to know?"

49

We didn't get much from Mr. Kragh, who was slick and slithered his way out of any question that wasn't about Leonora's work. He painted a very nice picture of a hard worker and a nice girl, who didn't stand out much in the crowd, but did as she was told. One of the rising young stars in the company.

But, after we left his office, we had a very good chat with the secretary.

"She did have an ex-boyfriend, who was sick with jealousy," she said, when we asked if she knew anything about her personal life.

"Really?"

"Yes. He would come to her place every now and then and attack her. He was jealous because she had found someone else."

"And, who was that?" I asked.

The secretary shook her head. She seemed to suddenly have to go. "I...it doesn't matter," she said, and her eyes landed on the door to Mr. Kragh's office.

"I see," I said.

"No, you can't write that," she said. "Morten will kill me."

"Oh, I won't. No need to worry," I said.

She put a hand to her chest. "Ah, good."

"But he is married, isn't he?"

"Yes," she said whispering. "The poor girl thought he was going to leave his wife, but he never intended to. She's not the first, you know. I've seen it so many times before."

I nodded and looked at the wall behind her. A big picture of Morten Kragh was displayed for everyone to see as the first thing when they approached the counter. Next to it was an empty spot, but the wood wasn't faded like the rest of the wall.

"What used to be on the wall there?" I asked.

The secretary turned. "Oh that. There used to hang a picture of Mr. Toft."

My eyes widened. "Mr. Toft as in Dan Toft?"

The secretary looked sad. "Yes," she said sniffling. "So tragic."

"So this company used to be Kragh & Toft?" I said, and looked at the logo, where I could tell the last part of the name had been removed.

The secretary sniffled again. "Yes. They had been partners for so many years. We miss him around here. He was the good one, if you know what I mean."

"Say, you wouldn't happen to know anything about where his children are these days, would you?" David asked.

"Dan's children?" she asked. "The twins?"

"Yes. We're looking for them."

She shook her head. "No. We haven't seen either of them for years. They both ran away from home when they were sixteen. I don't believe they had any contact at all with them after that. It was all very tragic."

"Okay," I said, a little disappointed. "I think we have what we came for. Thank you so much."

I was about to turn around and walk away, when I looked at her again.

"Do you happen to know the name of Leonora's ex-boyfriend?" I asked.

"Yes. His name is Henrik Pedersen. He's a cop."

"Do you know if Henrik knew Dan Toft from somewhere?" I asked.

"I don't believe they knew each other at all, no."

"I know this is going to sound strange, but do you know how Leonora felt about homosexuals?"

The secretary wrinkled her forehead. "About homosexuals? I don't think she had any issues with them. Her younger brother is gay. Came out of the closet just two years ago. She loved him more than anyone."

"Okay. Thank you."

"You're welcome."

In the car on the way back to the office, I couldn't keep my thoughts from flickering in my head. A lot of new information had appeared, but it didn't seem like there was any silver lining here. Henrik Pedersen had a baton. He could have killed Leonora in an attack of rage because she was with someone else. That was obvious. But why would he kill Dan and Tina Toft? Why would he kill the therapist or the pastor? And what about the clothes and the mutilated genitals?

It made no sense.

50

"Maybe he thought Leonora was having an affair with Dan Toft and not that Kragh guy?" David asked, when we were back at the office eating lunch.

We had been discussing Henrik Pedersen and his possible motives ever since we got back, and I hadn't been able to write a single word on my article yet. I simply couldn't focus.

"You're thinking he knew she was seeing one of the partners and then killed the wrong one. That could be a motive," I said, my mouth filled with herring. "But it doesn't explain the wife, the therapist, or the pastor."

"Could Henrik Pedersen be Hans Toft? Could he have changed his name?" Sara asked.

"It's a possibility. But the secretary knew him. She would have known if Henrik were Dan's son. She would have recognized him," I said. "Besides, he told me he grew up on my street. He could be lying about that, but why should he?"

"True," David said. He drank his soda.

"Okay, so what do we know? The twins. The sister had identity issues," I continued, and found the picture in my pocket. I stared at the young girl, who looked like she was trying to hide from the world behind her long hair. "According to the neighbors, she wanted to look like a boy. If she was transgender, the story doesn't tell yet. But we know she was being bullied."

I paused and thought for a little while. I drew on a piece of paper and wrote the names of the people who had been killed. "She could have been one of Dr. Korner's patients. We were told he had this program where they tried to help children." I rubbed my forehead in frustration. "The pastor was against homosexuals. Maybe the killer is just killing people who are against homosexuals?"

"Like a reverse hate crime?" David said.

"Something like that. But where does Leonora fit into this category?"

David leaned back in his chair with a sigh. "She's clearly not a lesbian; she's not anti-homosexual either. It makes no sense."

Sara served us coffee and cookies after lunch, and I started writing my article about the hardworking rising star in the law firm, and then another about how this serial killer now had killed a second person in the same firm. I wasn't sure I was going to publish that one until I had confirmed that she was killed by the same killer, and I needed Sune to get that confirmation. Only he could give me access to the autopsy file.

"Maybe she wasn't killed by the serial killer after all?" I said, and looked at David. "What if Henrik Pedersen took advantage of all these killings and made a copy, so no one would suspect him?"

"There would still be differences in the way it was performed," David said. "Copycats can be accurate, but never completely the same. We need access to that file. You're sure you can't get ahold of Sune?" he asked.

I looked at my phone. Not even a text from him all day. He

had threatened to move out. Was that really what he had done? Was it that easy for him to simply cut me off?

"I can try and call him," I said.

David nodded. "Tell him we really need him."

I sighed and picked up the phone. I found his name and pressed the button. It started ringing. I looked at Sara, who bit her lip with anxiety.

"How are we on finding the twins?" I asked.

"I've been in contact with thirty-three men with the name Hans Toft so far, but haven't found the right one yet."

"Keep it up. I want to find this guy or his sister. At least to give them the picture."

"I will."

"Hello?"

It was Sune. My heart stopped.

"Rebekka?"

"Hey, it's me. Did I wake you up?"

"At one in the afternoon? How old do you think I am?"

"I'm sorry. You just sounded so tired, that's all."

"Well, I've been busy all day searching for apartments. Guess I am tired. I didn't sleep at all last night."

"Me either. Listen, I…"

"Could you find background information on Henrik Pedersen?" David asked Sara in the background. Sune went quiet.

Uh-oh.

"Are you at the office? Was that David?"

"Yes."

Sune took in a deep breath. "So, he's replaced me completely, has he?"

"I…I didn't think you…"

"No, that's great. Thank you," he said and hung up.

51

"So, is Sune coming?" Sara asked. She knew the answer right away when she saw my face.

"Guess not," she said, and sat down at her desk.

I pushed back my tears. I was getting so tired of being sad and angry at Sune. I couldn't do anything right in this, so maybe it was time to just move on.

"I'll just revise the article," I said. "I'll write that it isn't confirmed yet that Leonora was killed by the same killer. But there's still a story about two people being killed from the same firm. Jens-Ole will like that."

"What about this Kragh guy?" David said, tapping his pencil rhythmically on the table.

"What about him?"

David shrugged. "He has a motive for killing his partner and taking over the company, and for killing the girl, since he had slept with her through the years and now he wanted to get rid of her."

I shrugged too. "I guess it's a motive, even if it's a little farfetched."

"Maybe Leonora threatened to tell his wife? Maybe she was pregnant?" Sara said.

"You watch way too many soaps," I said, laughing. "I guess Hans Toft had a face transplant as well, so that's why he could come back with a new identity and no one recognized him?"

Sara chuckled. "It could happen, you know? I heard they do some very good ones in Sweden and South Korea."

I shook my head and returned to my screen while Sara's phone rang. This was too far out even for me. I had to admit I liked the theory of the lawyer guy. I didn't like him one bit from the moment I saw him. And he did have a motive. I wondered if the police had looked closely at him. Only Sune could help me answer that and...well, I wasn't going to count on him anymore. I had to figure out a way to get my stories on my own, at least for now.

"What about the fact that he was supposed to be a policeman?" I suddenly blurted out.

David looked at me. Sara was busy chatting on the phone.

"It was the theory in the beginning, remember?" I continued. "I even wrote an article telling how hard it was to get a hold of a real baton. That sure puts Henrik Pedersen in the hot seat, doesn't it?"

"I just got some info about him," Sara said, and put the phone down.

"He grew up here in Karrebaeksminde," I said. "That much I know. He told me we went to the same school. We even lived on the same street."

"He did grow up here," Sara said. "But so did I, and as you probably know by now, I know some people around here. I've asked around a little. And we have some mutual friends. One of them just called me back and told me that Henrik is well known in the gay circles around town. He is often seen at Pan's. The town's only gay bar."

I shook my head. "But that makes no sense. He was madly in love with Leonora?"

"No. He's not gay. But his sister is. A couple of years ago, she was the victim of an ugly hate crime that left her beaten half to death. It happened right after she had left the bar. Today, she lives in an institution for the handicapped. Henrik has since taken it upon himself to keep the streets and bars safe for the gays. He parades in there, wearing his uniform, every Friday and Saturday night. The bar likes to have him there. It makes the guests feel safe."

"Wow, that's a sad story," I said.

"I know," Sara replied.

I looked at David. "Sure gives him motive, though."

"The best one we've seen yet."

"Let's go talk to him. Feel him out a little," I said, and grabbed my jacket.

"With pleasure," David said, and followed.

52

We found Henrik Pedersen at the police station downtown. He was sitting behind his desk with his legs up, drinking coffee, and playing candy crush. He smiled and sat up straight when he saw us.

"Rebekka? What a great surprise."

"Well, we were just in the neighborhood and wanted to see how the investigation was going." I looked at the screen. "I see you're working hard."

Henrik Pedersen blushed and removed the game. "I was just on a little break. Besides, I'm not investigating, you know that. That's not my field."

"I know. We were just thinking about the case with the five killings, and wondered if you had looked into the gay angle?"

Henrik Pedersen looked perplexed. "What do you mean?"

"The pastor was speaking out against homosexuals. The therapist had a program where they apparently thought they could turn kids away from being gay with the right influences. I don't know the details, but something like that. The Toft couple had a daughter who was gay that they wouldn't accept."

Henrik Pedersen nodded pensively. It looked like it was the first he'd heard of it. "I see. That is an interesting angle. But how does Leonora fit in that?"

Bingo. So, Leonora was killed by the same killer.

"That's the only one that is unaccounted for. But it fits with the killer's desire to dress up his victims like the opposite sex and mutilate the genitals to make them genderless, right?"

Henrik Pedersen leaned back in his chair. "I...I don't think anyone has thought of that."

"Really? Not even you, Officer Pedersen?"

He shook his head. "No. Now, we're not supposed to talk about the case with the press, but I'll drop a word with the investigators about this. I don't have to let them know where it came from. They need to know the connection."

He was a good actor.

My eyes dropped to his belt. "So, you found your baton, I see?"

"What? Oh, yeah. That day I didn't bring it, I'd left it in my car. Silly me."

"Could I see it?"

He stared at me like I had asked if I could marry his sister.

"It's just...well, I've never held one of those and I really wanted to feel it in my hands. I know it's a little strange to ask."

Henrik Pedersen smiled. I could tell he liked me. I used it.

"No. That's okay." He pulled out his baton and I held it in my hand.

It was so much heavier than I had imagined. I tried to picture it hitting someone in the head.

"Probably wouldn't take more than one hit to knock someone out, huh?" I handed it back, and he put it on his belt.

"That's kind of the idea," he said.

"Of course it is. Have you ever used yours?" I asked.

"It happens. When you have to separate people in a bar fight, for instance."

I stared at Officer Pedersen. I was scrutinizing him, trying hard to see if he was just a very good liar. I hated the fact that he seemed so sympathetic. He had, after all, made life a living hell for his ex-girlfriend. But then, he also acted as the homosexuals' protector in the nightlife. Was he a superhero or a serial killer? I couldn't decide. He was kind of creepy as well.

"Anything else I can do for you two?" he asked.

I looked at David, and then shook my head. "No, I think we're done here."

"Well, give me a call sometime," he said, and handed me his card.

I stared at the card, then up at him. He blushed.

"Just in case you come up with any new theories that we should take a look at," he said with a shy smile.

53

I PICKED up the kids a little early that afternoon, thinking they deserved it, since I had been late so many times. We had tea in the kitchen with my dad and ate cookies. The mood around the table was low, and I tried to cheer them up by talking about how it would soon be spring, and then we were going to play in the yard again, maybe go out on one of our friend's boats. But it didn't seem to help. Besides, we all knew spring was months away, and darkness still reigned outside.

"When do you think my dad will be back?" Tobias asked, looking so sad it almost hurt.

I hated what this was doing to him, to all of them. William was fussing, and I let him down from his chair. "I don't know, Tobias. I talked to him earlier, and he told me he was looking for a place for the two of you."

Julie let out a shriek. "What? They're moving out?"

"We don't know yet, but yes, that might be the consequence. Sune and I aren't getting along very well, and think that maybe a little time apart will help things get better."

Julie's eyes filled up. "But…But…I love Sune. I love Tobias. I don't want to live apart. What about William?"

I put a hand on her shoulder to try and calm her down. "Take it easy, now. We'll figure all those things out. Don't you worry about any of it. You'll still get to see Tobias. Maybe you can also go on weekends there when William goes. We'll figure it out."

Julie was crying now. "I hate this!" she said, slamming her plate onto the table. "I hate you!"

Then she stormed out of the kitchen and up the stairs. Tobias ran after her. I could hear their angry steps on the stairs.

Damn you, Sune!

I felt my dad's hand on my shoulder. Now he was trying to comfort me.

"Let her process it. She's entitled to be angry for a little while. Then, go talk to her. She'll be fine."

"I just hate doing this to her again. To them. It's not fair."

"It's not all your fault," he said. "I must say, I find Sune a little cowardly for not being here when you broke the news."

"Well, he didn't know," I said. "I kind of just blurted it out. We haven't talked it over yet. We don't speak at all. He's shutting me completely out, Dad. He won't listen to anything I have to say. I had to tell them something, right?"

My dad nodded and put his arm around my shoulder. "He'll come around. Give him time. Sune is a good guy."

I sniffled and looked at my dad. What on earth would I ever do without him? Maybe I wasn't staying in his house because he needed it as much as because I needed him?

My phone vibrated in my pocket and I picked it up. My heart stopped.

"It's him," I said.

"Well, pick it up."

"Hello? Sune?" I said.

"I found a place to stay. We'll be able to move in next week.

I'll stay here till then, and Tobias can stay with you or come here to live with us. It's up to you."

I sighed. My hands started shaking. It was suddenly so real. "So, that's it, huh? Is it that easy for you to just leave us?"

"You have yourself to thank for that, Rebekka. You kept pushing me out. I can't be treated like a child for the rest of my life."

"You're not even willing to talk it over? We miss you here. I miss you."

He sighed again. "I miss you too, Rebekka. Goddammit. You don't make it easy. Hell, I love you, but..."

"I love you too. Isn't that worth working for? Come home, Sune. Let's talk instead." I wanted to say something about Jeppe and tell him the truth about what had happened in William's bedroom, about how he had sent me those creepy texts...to make Sune understand, but I hesitated. I was so afraid he wouldn't listen, that he would just get angry again.

"I...I can't...Not now at least. Now, do you want Tobias to stay with you or not? I know he'd prefer to live with you as long as possible. Besides, Jeppe's place isn't exactly suitable for children."

I hid my face in my hand and started crying. "Sure," I said through tears. "He can stay as long as he wants."

54

THE MAN WAS EXCITED. Everything was going the way he wanted it to. Leonora was gone. Got what she deserved, *the bitch*. The newspapers were filled with pictures of her and packed with questions as to why anyone would kill someone like her.

Such a beautiful young woman with such a promising career ahead of her. What a shame.

He knew the journalist lady was onto him. That Rebekka Franck woman. She was close, but she wouldn't be able to stop him. Not in time, at least.

"So, what do you say, Alex?" he asked his reflection.

"I'm so proud of you," his reflection spoke back.

The man smiled. It felt so good. Justice had served the people who had hurt them. He felt his baton on his belt. He liked holding it and took it out. He liked the weight of it. So much power in one little stick.

The power of life and death.

The man looked at the newspaper again, with Leonora's picture on the front. He had kind of gotten to like seeing his work in the papers. It gave him a sense of satisfaction. Of being someone. He mattered. He had a cause, and the people were going to understand his message. Not yet. Not now. But, one day, they would. When he had finished his work.

The man touched his reflection. A tear left his eye. "I'm sorry, Alex. I'm sorry for everything that happened to you. I'm so sorry!"

He grabbed the newspaper and held it up, so his reflection could see it. "You see? She got what she deserved. They all did."

The man sobbed, thinking about how unfair it had been, how badly everyone had treated his sister while growing up. He could hear her screaming inside his head, and held his hands to his ears to block it out.

I'm not a girl! I don't want to be a girl. I want to shave. I want to shoot guns. I want to cut my hair. Why won't they let me be who I am? Just leave me alone!

He remembered the day when she had dressed up in their father's suit after school and put her hair up under a hat, just as their father had walked in. Oh, how he remembered it. How their father had grabbed Alex in his arms and thrown her in the bathroom, where he had stripped her down and tied her hands with his belt, then beat the crap out of her with the whip that the pastor had given them. Alex had screamed and cried.

"I'm a boy! I'm a boy!"

Four hours the man had listened to his sister being beaten and screaming. Until she suddenly went quiet and their father came out of the bathroom, all sweating and red in the face. He had caught a glimpse of his sister inside the bathroom, her back striped in blood. The anger he had felt towards his parents at that instant filled him with such hatred he would never look at them the same way he used to again. That night, in their bedroom, while stroking his sister's hair to make her fall asleep, he swore they would one day pay for what they had done. They had made a pact back then, the two of them. A pact to get out of there, to escape before their parents drove them crazy. Before it was too late. The man had saved his money from being a newspaper boy. He had put it all away in a shoebox. Along with all the birthday money and the money he had saved up from the tooth fairy; they could get by for a little while. It had to work. It simply had to. It was their only chance.

The next day, their parents had taken Alex away and put her in that mental hospital. They told the man his sister was sick. They called it schizophrenia. When she returned, she was never the same. They had destroyed her. Broken her. And all their plans were gone. All their dreams for the future vanished. She wasn't his sister anymore. The girl who returned was someone else.

The man touched his reflection and cried at the memories.

"I'm so sorry I let them do this to you. I am so, so sorry."

55

I couldn't sleep. I kept tossing and turning in my bed, being either too hot or too cold. The bed felt so empty without Sune in it. I cried a lot and hit my face on the pillow, while cursing him and begging him to come back at the same time.

He said he loved you. He said he still loved you. Maybe there's still hope? But, why would he choose to move out if he still loved you? Why would he get a place of his own? I don't understand what I did wrong.

"Just come back," I whispered, while staring at the ceiling. It was a full moon outside and one of those freezing crystal clear nights. The light from the moon lit up parts of my bedroom through the curtain.

I looked at my phone one last time around two o'clock, hoping he would have texted me, but he hadn't. After that, I finally dozed off into an uneasy sleep.

I dreamt of Sune. Of course I dreamt about him. He was all I had on my mind. I dreamt we had taken a trip together. Just the two of us. It looked like Egypt, but we kept saying we were in Germany for some reason. It didn't look anything like Germany. It looked like the place in Egypt where I had been with Peter and Julie many years ago. But it didn't matter. What mattered was us. It was just us. There was no one else in the resort, or even in the world. The ocean was crystal clear and very blue. We went snorkeling. Sune was laughing. I was laughing. We were swimming in the pool, drinking in the bar, and dancing while walking back to our hotel room. We were hanging out on the balcony, drinking champagne and only having eyes for one another. At night, we made passionate love in the bedroom. My longing to feel him close to me was so real.

I was crying in my sleep, when suddenly, I felt someone in the bed with me. A warm naked body. Thinking I was still dreaming, I moaned and crept closer. It felt so good.

"Sune," I moaned.

"Mmmm," he moaned back.

I felt hands on my thighs, creeping up towards my panties. I reached out and grabbed his face, then moved up and touched his Mohawk. I pulled him closer as my desire for him rose.

"Sune," I mumbled again, while slowly waking up. I couldn't believe this. Had he come back? Had he really come back to me?

His hands were touching my breasts now. Caressing my stomach. He was kissing my neck and chest and moaning deeply. I felt his hand in my panties and they were pulled off. I smiled and pulled him closer. I was still crying; tears were slowly rolling across my cheeks. I had never wanted him more. I had never desired Sune more than in this second.

My T-shirt was pulled off and his lips were soon on my breasts. I closed my eyes and enjoyed his touches. He was getting hard now. I felt him, and he moaned in my ear. Then he kissed my breasts again and sucked on my nipples before he went further down. A chill when through my body and I shivered with excitement. Sune's tongue caressed me, and I moaned deeply with pleasure. I couldn't restrain myself. I had to come with a loud orgasm.

"Oh, my God, Sune!"

The waves of orgasm rolled through my body and made me forget everything, every tension, and every fight we ever had. For a few seconds, I felt better than I had in months, since I fell into the sinkhole in October. But it was just for a few wonderful seconds.

As the waves of excitement slowly vanished, I looked down, just as the light from the moon fell on Sune's face. The sight that met me was beyond terrifying. The eyes looking back at me didn't belong to Sune. The man looking back at me from between my naked legs wasn't Sune.

It was Jeppe.

56

I SCREAMED and kicked Jeppe in the face, so he fell backwards onto the floor. I grabbed a blanket and pulled it over me to cover myself up, then turned the light on.

"What the hell are you doing here?" I grunted. I could have killed him right there. Who the hell did he think he was? Why was he pretending to be Sune?

Jeppe laughed and got up from the floor. He was standing in front of me, naked and hard.

"You've got to be kidding me?" I yelled.

He walked closer. He had something in his hand.

It was a police baton. He looked down at his crotch.

"As you can tell, I'm not quite done yet," he said with a grin. "Now, come here and let me finish what I came here for. If you act nice, I won't hurt you…well, not too much at least."

I whimpered and pulled the blanket closer. I looked at my phone on the table next to my bed. I could try and go for it. I looked at Jeppe, walking closer. His engorged penis seemed almost unnaturally big. A vein was pumping in his forehead. He was clenching his jaw.

"Please, don't hurt me," I said, and took one more glance at the phone. Could I reach it and press something, maybe make a call to the alarm central before he could get to me?

"Now, that's not fair. You know I can't promise that," he said.

I glanced at him, then at the phone, and made a jump for it. I managed to grab it, but Jeppe was fast, and soon he was on top of me, holding me down. He grabbed my hands while I fought to press a button, anything, when he slammed my hand into the table, causing the phone to fall to the floor. I tried to push him off of me, to punch him and kick him, but he was strong. I managed to get one kick in that forced him backwards slightly, then I jumped out of bed, but Jeppe grabbed my foot mid-air and pulled me forcefully back. I hit my chest on the edge of the bed and it knocked the air out of me.

"You sure have a nice piece of ass," he said, and caressed my behind gently.

I felt the baton roll over it. Its cold surface made me shiver. I caught my breath while he played with the baton on top of me, letting it drop a few times like he was spanking me. It hurt.

"Ouch!"

"Quiet!" he yelled.

Jeppe crept on top of my back and sat on me. He leaned down and whispered in my ear. "You're mine to play with now. Do everything I tell you to or I'll kill you. It's as simple as that."

"Let me go," I cried.

"Sorry, but I can't. See, I need you to get out of Sune's life, so he and I can move on. You're constantly on his mind, and I can't have that. I want him for myself. You're in our way. I need him. Alex and I are going to be happy again."

"Who the hell is Alex?" I grunted, while trying to get free from his grasp.

I didn't see it happen, but I sure felt it. The baton hit the back of my head so hard I almost lost consciousness immediately.

"Stop with the questions!" Jeppe yelled.

I screamed. The blow made me dizzy, and I felt like I had to throw up. I fought hard to not doze off, when suddenly, the door to the bedroom opened. Sune stood in the opening, holding a gun and pointing it at Jeppe.

"Get off of her now! Get down!"

I felt the weight disappear from my back, and in my dizziness, I saw Jeppe walk away with his hands held up in the air. The gun was shaking crazily in Sune's hands. He hated guns more than anything in this world, and I knew he had never held one before.

"Sune?" I said, in the seconds before everything turned into a myriad of stars.

57

WHEN I WOKE UP, I was lying on the bed. Sune was sitting on a chair next to me, holding his head between his hands.

"Sune?"

"Shh, lay still. I called for an ambulance. They're on their way."

"How...?" I tried to sit up, but had to lay back down. "Where's Jeppe?"

That was when I noticed the big bruise on Sune's forehead. He was bleeding and holding a wet cloth to it. Sune sighed.

"I lost him. He ran off. I'm sorry, Rebekka. I'm such a coward. Jeppe called me out. He knew I was bluffing. He grabbed that lamp you see on the floor down there with my blood on it and asked me to shoot him. Slowly, he walked closer while I yelled at him to get back. Of course, I couldn't shoot him. I could never shoot anyone. So he swung the lamp and knocked me out. He took the gun and ran."

"I'm sorry you were hurt," I said, and reached out my hand. Sune grabbed it. "But you're no coward. You're just not a killer."

Sune looked at me and smiled. "I'm so sorry. You were

right about him all along. I had no idea. I thought you were just against me having fun. And, I guess I was slightly upset with the fact that I can't even provide for my own family, let alone give them a real home of their own. I felt emasculated. It was stupid. I can't believe he was such a creep."

I closed my eyes for a second to get the dizziness to go away. My head was spinning and hurting like crazy. My hands were shaking. Seconds later, it seemed to get better. I looked at Sune again.

"I'm surprised he didn't kill the both of us," I said.

"Well, your dad came to our rescue. After Jeppe knocked me down, he was about to shoot both of us, but your dad was suddenly in the door holding a rifle and pointing it at him. Did you know he had a rifle?"

"It's an old one from back when he used to go hunting. I don't think it even works anymore."

"Oh, it works alright. Your dad shot Jeppe in the foot. Jeppe screamed, then ran towards your dad and pushed him aside. He ran out and down the stairs."

"Oh, my God. Is my dad alright?"

"Yes. He says he didn't even hurt himself. I helped him get back to his bed."

"And the kids?"

"They're fine. Tobias was the only one who woke up from the shot. I put him back to bed. William and Julie slept through everything." Sune scoffed. "I can't believe I didn't see this coming. Why didn't I listen to you? I put all of you in danger."

"True. But you also saved us. I can't even dare to think about what would have happened if you hadn't come. How did you know we were in trouble?"

"It was the weirdest thing. Jeppe had been acting strange all day. It was like he didn't want me to get an apartment. He helped me look at places, but none were good enough. He was trying to get me to stay with him instead, and he kept calling me Alex. He talked to me like we had known each other for years, like we were brothers. It got really creepy. I had never noticed it before, but sometimes it's like he slips into another world, if you know what I mean. He pauses when he speaks, and then it's like he's gone for a little while, and when he returns he acts differently. I don't know how to explain it, but I don't think he's well."

"I think we can agree on that," I said, and chuckled, but it hurt my head. Sune smiled and kissed me. He looked into my eyes.

"He tried so hard to get me to forget about you, and he kept telling me that, finally, we were all alone, and it started to freak me out. I went to bed early, but woke up around one o'clock, when I heard Jeppe walking around in the living room. I snuck closer and watched him as he talked to himself in the mirror...dressed in his uniform in the middle of the night."

"He's a police officer?" I said.

"I thought you knew. He works with Naestved Police Department."

"But, he never seemed to work?" I asked.

"Well, he had taken two weeks off to move. But I did see him leave his house in his uniform a couple of times this week anyway, so maybe he did go to work after all. He also left me several times at the café during the day, telling me he had to work for a few hours. I never thought much about it, but now I do. Anyway, I watched him talk to his own reflection, and then he left the house. At first, I thought I'd just go back to bed, so I went back to my room, but through my window, I saw him walk to our house. I saw him open the back door with a key. I guess he must have stolen my key and made a copy or something."

"My dad keeps extra keys in his drawer downstairs in the

hallway because, in my family, we constantly lose our keys. Not very safe, but what can you do? It would only take Jeppe a few minutes alone downstairs to find them."

"That makes sense. So, he was here that night when you saw him looking at us. I guess he must have used that same key." Sune shivered and looked at me. "When I saw him walk into your dad's house, I was terrified. Suddenly, I realized that everything you had told me was true. I feared for you and the kids, but had no idea how to stop him. I searched the entire house for a weapon, anything I could use in case I needed it, and finally I found the gun in his closet. I'm surprised he has both his baton and gun in his house, since officers are supposed to leave all that at the station when they leave."

"Guess Jeppe doesn't play by the rules," I said. "Did you call the police?"

"Yes. I talked to Henrik Pedersen, who was on duty, and they have all the patrols looking for him. He won't get far."

58

I SPENT the rest of the night in the hospital, while the doctors checked me and held me under observation for a concussion. I felt great after a few hours, but they insisted on keeping me, so I wasn't going to take any chances.

Sune was being checked on too, but they released him after just a few hours, and he stayed by my side through every examination and waiting period. My dad had promised to take care of the kids. I called Anne-Marie, Julie's best friend's mother and asked her to help get the kids to school and William to his day-care. When she heard what happened, she told me not to worry.

"I'll take care of everything," she said.

The police came to my bedside and asked me a ton of questions. They still hadn't found Jeppe, they told me, but they were doing all they could.

Henrik Pedersen told me to get better soon and to contact him in case I needed anything. "This case is very close to my heart," he said. "We'll get the bastard. Don't worry about it."

"I think the officer has a little crush on you," Sune said, when Officer Pedersen had left.

"Oh, my goodness," I said, and held a hand to my head. It still hurt when I laughed, but not as bad as earlier.

"I just wish they would get the creep, you know?" Sune said. "It's not like this town is that big. There are only so many places for a guy with a green Mohawk to hide."

"You should know…" I paused and looked intently at him. "Wasn't there another doctor?"

"What was that?" Sune asked.

I sat up. My head didn't hurt anymore. "There was. What was his name again? He was working with Dr. Korner on those children. The secretary told us. Dr.…Dr. I have it on the tip of my tongue. Dr. Winter! Yes, that was it. His name was Dr. Winter."

I grabbed my phone and called Sara.

"I need you to find Dr. Winter for me," I said, without any explanation.

"Well, hello to you too, Rebekka," she answered. "Getting better, I reckon?" I heard her tap on her computer. "Here. That was easy. Dr. Winter is retired now and lives on Enoe. On Enoe Kystvej. Nice address."

"Enoe Kystvej," I repeated, while taking off my covers and signaling Sune, who looked like he didn't understand anything. "What number?"

"Sixteen."

"Great, thanks," I said, and hung up.

I looked at Sune. He shook his head. "No, Rebekka. You're in here for observation, remember?"

I swung my legs out of the bed. "Give me the bag with my clothes."

"Rebekka!"

"What?"

"You're hurt. Lie down and rest. Tell the police what you're thinking. Let them take care of it."

Just as he spoke, the doctor entered the room. He was

smiling. That was a good sign. "All the tests were perfect, Rebekka. You're good to go. We're done with you. Just make sure you get proper rest over the coming days."

I jumped out of bed and grabbed my bag of clothes. "I will, Doctor. Don't worry about it."

I got dressed as soon as the doctor left and looked at Sune. "I want to talk to this doctor. I have a feeling he holds the key to this story. We've made it this far. Don't let it be for nothing. I want answers."

59

"Dr. Winter?"

The old man looked at me like he was confused. He was standing in the doorway of his house, which was located on the beach of Enoe, one of the most beautiful places you could live in our area, at least that's how I felt. I had always dreamt of living in one of these houses on the beach.

"Yes? Who are you?" the old man asked.

I reached out my hand. "My name is Rebekka Franck. This is Sune Johansen. We work for *Zeeland Times*. Could we talk with you for a second?"

"Rebekka Franck? I know you. I read your stories in my paper all the time. What on earth do you want to talk to me about?"

"The Toft family," I said.

Dr. Winter looked down. "Ah, them. Well, I guess there's no harm in that. Come on in."

We followed him into the living room, where we sat on the couch looking out at the ocean. It was gorgeous. Breathtaking even. It suddenly occurred to me that I did want a house of my own. I wanted a place I could decorate the way I wanted to, a place that was ours, just ours, just Sune's and mine. I wanted a house like this one.

"It's such an old story," the doctor said with a sigh.

"I know. But we would like to know it. We would like to hear your side of it. Please. We want to know what happened to Alex and Hans Toft."

The doctor smiled. "I ran this program under the title *Gender reassignment*. Basically, we tried to prove that gender isn't something you are born with, it is taught and could be altered by the nature of what you are exposed to during childhood. So parents came to us if their children suffered from what we called *gender confusion,* like if their little boy dressed up as a girl or vice versa. We tried to influence them in the right way. Basically, to make life easier for them."

"So you tried to reprogram gays?" I asked, wondering how people could be so ignorant still, even back in the nineties.

The doctor snorted. "They weren't necessarily gay. More like what we today would call transgender. In my opinion, they were simply confused. We tried to help them."

"You and Dr. Korner?" I asked.

"Yes. We did a big research program and published it. It was quite the big deal back then."

"So, at what point did Tina and Dan Toft approach you?"

The doctor cleared his throat. "Well, they had troubles with their daughter Alexandra…"

"Alex," Sune said.

"Yes, she preferred to be called Alex. The poor girl lived under the conviction that she was really a boy. So, we tried to help her in any way we could. She became a huge part of our research project. You can read all about it in our thesis. It was published in many medical journals all over the world. We did some groundbreaking research."

"I bet you did," I said, wondering what all this research had done to the poor little girl. I was starting to get annoyed with this guy. I hated doctors who thought they were gods.

"So, what happened to the twins? All we know is that they ran away from home," I said.

The doctor's face froze. He stared at me, looking like he was figuring out what to say. "She was admitted to a mental institution," he said. "She suffered from severe schizophrenia. She committed suicide when she went home." The doctor sighed and shook his head. "It was tragic. She wasn't well. Somehow, she had gotten ahold of a pair of scissors and… well. The parents told me."

"But the neighbors told us they ran away?" I asked.

"Well, the parents never told anyone what had really happened. Guess they were too afraid of what the neighbors would think. The boy did run away from home. I guess he blamed his parents for her suicide. Anyway, that's all I know."

I pulled out the photo given to me by the neighbor and looked at it. I felt so bad for the poor girl. The suicide gave Hans Toft the motive. I looked at Sune. "Do you have a picture of Jeppe?"

Sune shrugged. "I might have one in my phone, why?"

"Show it to Dr. Winter, will you please?"

"Sure." Sune flipped through his pictures, then found one of him and Jeppe at the Internet Café and showed it to him.

"Is this Hans Toft?" I asked.

The doctor put on his glasses and looked at the photo. "Yes, that's him," he said. "I think…but, wait a second. The mole." He looked at the picture once again, then at me from above his glasses. "That is not Hans Toft," he said.

60

ALEX TOFT HAD HEARD everything from behind the door. He had entered the doctor's house through an open window in the basement, and now he was watching them through the door leading to the kitchen. He was sweating heavily and trying hard to restrain himself from just walking in there and shooting all of them. He knew that he would have to at some point.

But it had to be at the right time.

"Look at the mole," the old doctor said. Alex could see him through the crack in the door. He was pointing at the phone, and then at the picture the woman was holding.

If only you had killed her while you had the chance, you idiot!
Shut up, Hans.
You shut up, Alex! Stupid...

"The man in this picture has a mole on the right side of his nose, whereas the boy in this picture has the mole on the left side," the doctor continued. "There is no way this can be Hans Toft. It has to...I don't know how this can be, but it has to be Alexandra."

That's it. That's your cue!

Alex held the gun tightly between his hands, then took in a deep breath.

"Here goes nothing," he mumbled, right before he kicked the door to the living room. It shattered, and Alex walked inside, pointing the gun at the three people.

"You're absolutely right, dear Doctor," he said.

Their baffled faces were worth it all.

"Alexandra?" Dr. Winter said. He gasped and held a hand to his chest.

"At your service. Or, wait a minute. I think I have been for most of my LIFE!" Alex walked closer with the gun pointing directly at the doctor. He wanted to shoot right now, just finish him off. Just the sight of the doctor that had tortured him his entire childhood made him so angry he could hardly restrain himself. But, he had to. It wasn't over just yet. The doctor needed to pay.

"But...but how is this possible?" The doctor said, stuttering.

"I told you, dear Doctor. I told you numerous times." Alex walked closer and held the gun to the doctor's temple. The doctor whimpered. Alex leaned over and yelled in his face. "I am not a girl!"

"Jeppe, please," Sune said. "There's no need to hurt any more people."

Alex turned his head and stared at him. Then, he swung the gun and hit Sune with it. Sune fell backwards. The whiny Rebekka Franck started screaming.

"I thought you would be my brother," Alex said. "Now, you mean nothing to me."

Alex returned to the doctor and pressed the gun to his forehead again. "Now, dear Doctor, I would like to tell these nice people the entire story, if you don't mind. I think they deserve it, don't you?"

"What do you mean the entire story?" Rebekka Franck asked.

"Of course, you wouldn't tell them. Why should you do that, Doctor dear? But I can. I can tell them."

Rebekka Franck stared at Alex. He smiled. "All of my life, I was told I was a girl, when really I'm not."

"We know they didn't accept you…" Rebekka said.

"NO!" Alex yelled.

Rebekka jumped.

"It wasn't like that," Alex continued. "It wasn't that I thought I was a boy. I WAS a boy. I was originally born as a boy. Right, Doctor?"

Doctor Winter whimpered and nodded.

"See, my parents had twins," Alex said. "Twin brothers. But the doctors were supposed to perform a simple procedure when I was just a child. But something went wrong, didn't it? Didn't it, Doctor!"

"Y…yes. Yes, it did."

"Both my brother and I had problems urinating from birth. A simple circumcision would fix the problem, they told our parents. What should have been a routine operation destroyed my life. Rather than perform the operation with a blade, the surgeons used a faulty cauterizing needle. My brother went through the operation just fine, but the electrical equipment malfunctioned while I was on the operating table, leaving me with injuries to my genitals. I was burnt. My penis was gone. Months later, my parents still didn't know what to do with their disfigured son. Until they were introduced to Dr. Winter and Dr. Korner, who believed that nurture, rather than biology, was the significant factor in determining gender, and as it so happened to be, my brother and I represented the perfect opportunity to test the theory. The doctors' proposal was for me to be raised as a girl, alongside my twin brother. They couldn't recreate what had been burned, but they could surgically make me a girl. Under no circumstances was I to be told that I was really a boy. After yet another surgery, I became Alexandra. With hormones and the right influences, they were determined to make me a girl, no matter the cost. And, for years, it seemed that they'd succeeded. At least, according to the two doctors' thesis that they wrote and published, but they failed to mention how miserable my life was and how I constantly tried to tell the world that I didn't feel like a girl, even though everyone told me that's what I was. In the end, they all just decided I was CRAZY and admitted me."

"So...so, you killed your brother when you returned home? It was him they found, wasn't it?" Rebekka Franck asked.

"I stabbed him with a pair of scissors. I cut off his penis and he bled to death. I watched him all night as he died. I hated him for being everything I wanted to be. I hated them all. My parents, the pastor who told them to whip the defiance out of me, the doctors who tried to change me. When my brother died, so did Alexandra. Instead, I became him, I became my brother. I ran away. I used my brother's name until I changed it to Jeppe Kastberg, so no one in my family could ever find me. My parents never told anyone what really happened. Their daughter was dead, that was all they said to the few of their closest relatives. Their son had run away from home. It wasn't completely wrong. I think they believed it was less embarrassing that way. I didn't see them again until the day I killed them. They hardly recognized me. Years after I escaped, I went through another change. I cut my hair and worked the streets for years. You won't believe how much some men will pay to sleep with a girl that looks like a little boy. Finally, I had earned enough money to get a sex change. Lots of people in the streets do that. After six years of hormonal treatments and an operation, I was finally a boy again. Finally, I could be who I was supposed to be. I became a police officer, but could never forget my childhood. All my life, I had thought I was wrong. That everything about me was all wrong. Do you have any idea how that feels? Then, one day, I decided to get my files from the hospital, and in reading them, I learned that I had actually been born a boy. I had been right all along. I could never forgive. Nor could I find peace. I had to do something."

"So, you killed your parents?"

"It wasn't planned. It just happened. I wanted to visit them for the first time since I left, but when I got there and we sat on that couch in that house where it had all taken place, I simply snapped. I had worn my uniform to make them proud of me. To let them see that I had made something of myself. Something inside of me shattered when I remembered all this. I don't remember doing it, but I grabbed the baton and simply started beating them. The anger inside of me was let loose and I couldn't hold it back any longer. After that, there was no way back. I had to punish all of them."

"Why Leonora?" Rebekka Franck asked.

Alex turned and looked at her. A new wave of fury rushed over him. "Leonora?" he asked, while gritting his teeth. "The bitch broke my heart. She ripped it out and stepped on it. I loved her. She thought I was a lesbian, and humiliated me, the bitch. They all got what was coming to them." Alex felt tears roll across his cheeks, and wiped them with his arm. Why was he crying all of a sudden?

He turned and looked at the doctor, with his heart racing in his chest, racing with rage. "It all started with you. You and your ideas of *gender reassignment*." Alex pressed the gun hard into the doctor's forehead and put a finger on the trigger.

"So many lives destroyed, just because of you and your ideas!"

"Please, don't hurt me," the doctor pleaded. "I only tried to help. I never meant to hurt you. You must know that. Please, don't hurt me. You're not well. You have clearly lost contact with yourself and who you are. You need help, Alex. Don't hurt me. We can figure it out."

"I have to."

Alex looked into the eyes of the doctor one last time before he pulled the trigger.

61

I screamed as the gun went off, but it was drowned out by the sound of the blast. I watched as the bullet went through the doctor's head and slammed into the wall behind him, while blood spurted onto the white paint.

Alex Toft panted and was pushed backwards from the blow. As soon as he had regained his balance, he turned the gun to point it at Sune and me. I gasped and put my hands in the air.

"I'm sorry, Alex," I said. "For everything that has happened to you, but there is no need for anyone else to be hurt."

My voice was breaking. I was about to scream and cry at the same time. The terrifying image of the bullet going through the doctor's head kept flickering in my mind.

"Please, don't hurt us. We have children. You know them. They need us. You're angry, and I understand why, but please don't take it out on us. It's over, Alex. Everyone who hurt you back then is dead. Isn't it enough?"

Alex was sweating. His face was red with restraint. He gritted his teeth and panted while pointing the gun at us. In the distance, I could hear sirens. Someone had called the police, probably when they heard the gunshot. The sound filled me with hope.

"Alex, put the gun down," Sune said. He smiled and got up. I stared at Sune as he walked closer to Alex. "Come on. You and me, we're buddies, remember? We're like brothers. Hell, we could be twins. Look at how much we look like each other. Let's run away together. Everything will be like it used to. Just you and me. Brothers having fun. There will be no doctors, no parents, no teachers, and no deranged pastors. Just us. But we have to hurry before the police get here."

Alex stared at Sune. His hands were shaking. "What about her?" He nodded in my direction.

"She's unimportant," Sune said. "I left her, remember? I left her to be with you. Just like you wanted me to. I want to be with you instead. Never let a girl come between brothers, right? She's not important. Just leave her. Come on. Let's go."

Alex sniffled and looked at Sune. I could tell he really liked Sune, and hoped he liked him enough that he wouldn't want to hurt him. "Do you really mean that?" he said, sniffling.

"Yes. Of course I do. Now, come here." Sune reached out his arms. "Give your brother a hug. I miss you, man."

"No!" Alex yelled. "You're trying to trick me!"

"Look at me, Alex. Look into my eyes. I'm not trying to trick you. But the police will be here soon, and we need to hurry."

I heard the sirens come closer, then stop outside the house. Feet were running around the house. A face peeked in the window and spotted Alex with the gun.

"Come on, Alex," Sune said. "Give me a hug. It'll be like old times. I'm back."

Tears gushed across Alex's face. He was fighting within himself. "I've missed you, Hans," he said. Then, he lowered the gun and threw himself in Sune's arms. I breathed a sigh of relief, when suddenly the door was kicked in and officers stormed the room.

It all went by so fast I could hardly react. As the door was kicked in, I turned and watched as the officers pointed their guns at Alex. They were screaming at him to put down his weapon, then yelling at me to get to safety. I wanted to yell back that we had everything under control...that they shouldn't scare Alex, but I was too late.

I looked back at Alex, just in time to see him lift the gun, point it at Sune's stomach, and pull the trigger. Then, they shot him. Three guns went off at the same time, while Sune fell to the ground with a thud. Everything inside of me screamed.

NOOOOO!

EPILOGUE

Sune was on the operating table all night, while I waited desperately in the waiting room for news. Every sound and every person coming in or out of the room made me jump.

Finally, in the early morning, the doctor came to see me.

"It doesn't look good," he said.

My heart dropped. That was never something you wanted to hear from a doctor. "What do you mean, it doesn't look good?"

The doctor took in a deep breath. Another bad sign.

"He's alive and stable now. That's the good news."

"And the bad news?"

"He probably won't walk again. I'm sorry. I wish I had better news."

Oh, my God! This can't be real!

"Are you sure? I mean, what about rehabilitation programs?" I asked, desperately clinging to hope.

The doctor shook his head. "He's paralyzed from the waist down, Rebekka. There's nothing that can be done about it. The bullet hit him in his spinal column, the thoracic vertebra. It damaged his spine. I have to be honest and tell you he'll never be able to walk again."

And just like that, my life, our lives were changed forever. I had no one to talk to about it, since my dad was at home taking care of the kids. I fell into one of the chairs with a deep moan and started crying and sulking, simply devastated.

Just then, the door opened, and David entered along with Sara. "How is he?" David asked, as they approached me.

I threw myself in his arms. "David, oh, it's terrible!"

I hugged Sara and she held me tight. "What are the doctors saying?" she asked.

"He'll never walk again. The bullet damaged his spine."

"Oh, my God, Rebekka," David said. "I'm so sorry. Is there anything we can do for you?"

"I'll get you some coffee," Sara said. "And some chocolate maybe?"

"I'm not hungry, but coffee sure sounds nice," I said. "I've been here all night."

I sat back down and David sat next to me. "I'm so sorry, Rebekka," he repeated.

"He tried to save me. He tried to save us. He was being so brave."

David grabbed me and held me close to him while I cried. Sara brought us coffee, and later the doctor came back.

"He can see you now," he said.

I looked at David and Sara. They smiled and nodded me on. "Go on, Rebekka. We'll be here when you get back," Sara said, trying to smile. "Your dad is on his way with the kids, as well. I talked to them half an hour ago and they had just gotten in the cab."

Sune looked like a ghost when I entered his room. He had

tubes everywhere and was so pale he blended in with the pillow. He opened his eyes and looked at me. I could tell he was sad, but he tried to smile.

Oh, my God, he's trying to be brave for me!

"By the look on your face, I'm guessing they told you?" Sune said.

I nodded and grabbed his hand. It was so cold. I warmed it between mine. "You were so brave, Sune."

"I did alright, didn't I?"

"You definitely did. You saved our lives. I can't…I can't begin to explain how much…"

I couldn't finish the sentence. Tears burned my eyes. It was just so unfair. Why did he have to be the one who suffered? Why did he have to be the one to never walk again?

Sune's eyes grew sad. "Maybe it would have been better for all of us if I died, huh?"

I shook my head and kissed his hand. "No, Sune. Don't you ever say that! I wouldn't know how to live without you. We'll get through this. We'll get a house with no stairs. Maybe on the water like the doctor's, huh?"

He squeezed my hand and looked me intensely in the eyes. "I'm gonna prove them wrong, Rebekka."

I could hear the kids outside the room now. I swallowed the lump in my throat.

"But, honey…the doctor says that…"

The door opened and Tobias, Julie, and William stormed in, followed by my dad, who was leaning on his cane and panting heavily from the walk. Julie hugged me. She was holding William's hand. He staggered towards Sune, but fell to his behind.

"Daaad!" Tobias yelled and ran to him.

Sune put his arm around his son. His eyes didn't move from mine. He looked intently at me while he spoke.

"No, I'm serious, Rebekka. I *will* walk again. I will. I promise you."

I leaned over and kissed his forehead, while tears rolled across my cheeks. "If you say so, my love. If you say so."

THE END

DEAR READER,

Thank you for purchasing "Thirteen, Fourteen…Little Boy Unseen" (Rebekka Franck #7). I hope you enjoyed reading it. I'm sorry to leave Sune like this. I have to admit, I had no idea this was going to happen to him when I started writing this book. But it did. I promise we'll know a lot more about his and Rebekka's struggles in the coming books.

I have dedicated this book to my childhood friend Camilla. Growing up, Camilla was different than the rest of us girls. She loved skateboarding; she cut her hair short and looked like a boy. When she grew up, Camilla realized she no longer wanted to be a girl; she went through a sex change, and today she is a man. She even has a family with a wife and two children. If you saw him today you wouldn't be able to tell that he was born a girl. It's quite amazing. Naturally, he was a big inspiration for this story.

Furthermore, the twins' story in this book was also inspired by a true story. I know it sounds like it's too crazy to be true, but it isn't. It happened. Not in Denmark, but in the U.S. Here is an article about it, if you'd like to know more: http://www.dailymail.co.uk/news/article-1332396/Bruce-Reimer-Tragic-twin-boy-brought-girl.html

Don't forget to check out my other books if you haven't already read them. Just follow the links below. And don't forget to leave reviews, if you can.

Thank you,

AFTERWORD

Willow

Connect with Willow online and you will be the first to know about new releases and bargains from Willow Rose.
*Sign up to the **VIP** email here:*
http://eepurl.com/vVfEf
I promise not to share your email with anyone else, and I won't clutter your inbox. I'll only contact you when a new book is out or when I have a special bargain/free eBook.

Follow Willow Rose on BookBub:
https://www.bookbub.com/authors/willow-rose

BOOKS BY THE AUTHOR

MYSTERY/HORROR NOVELS

- In One Fell Swoop
- Umbrella Man
- Blackbird Fly
- To Hell in a Handbasket
- Edwina

7TH STREET CREW SERIES

- What Hurts the Most
- You Can Run
- You Can't Hide
- Careful Little Eyes

EMMA FROST SERIES

- Itsy Bitsy Spider
- Miss Dolly had a Dolly
- Run, Run as Fast as You Can
- Cross Your Heart and Hope to Die
- Peek-a-Boo I See You
- Tweedledum and Tweedledee
- Easy as One, Two, Three
- There's No Place like Home
- Slenderman
- Where the Wild Roses Grow

JACK RYDER SERIES

- Hit the Road Jack
- Slip out the Back Jack
- The House that Jack Built
- Black Jack

REBEKKA FRANCK SERIES

- One, Two…He is Coming for You
- Three, Four…Better Lock Your Door
- Five, Six…Grab your Crucifix
- Seven, Eight…Gonna Stay up Late
- Nine, Ten…Never Sleep Again
- Eleven, Twelve…Dig and Delve
- Thirteen, Fourteen…Little Boy Unseen

HORROR SHORT-STORIES

- Better watch out
- Eenie, Meenie
- Rock-a-Bye Baby
- Nibble, Nibble, Crunch
- Humpty Dumpty
- Chain Letter
- Mommy Dearest
- The Bird

PARANORMAL SUSPENSE/FANTASY NOVELS

AFTERLIFE SERIES

- Beyond

- Serenity
- Endurance
- Courageous

THE WOLFBOY CHRONICLES

- A Gypsy Song
- I am WOLF

DAUGHTERS OF THE JAGUAR

- Savage
- Broken

ABOUT THE AUTHOR

The Queen of Scream, Willow Rose, is an international best-selling author. She writes Mystery/Suspense/Horror, Paranormal Romance and Fantasy. She is inspired by authors like James Patterson, Agatha Christie, Stephen King, Anne Rice, and Isabel Allende. She lives on Florida's Space Coast with her husband and two daughters. When she is not writing or reading, you'll find her surfing and watching the dolphins play in the waves of the Atlantic Ocean. She has sold more than two million books.

Connect with Willow online:
willow-rose.net
madamewillowrose@gmail.com

WHAT HURTS THE MOST - EXCERPT

For a special sneak peak of Willow Rose's Mystery Novel
What hurts the most(*7th Street Crew*), turn to the next page.

PROLOGUE

COCOA BEACH 1995

THEY'RE NOT GOING to let her go. She knows they won't. Holly is terrified as she runs through the park. The sound of the waves is behind her. A once so calming sound now brings utter terror to her. She is wet. Her shirt is dripping, her shoes making a slobbering sound as she runs across the parking lot towards the playground.

Run, run! Don't look back. Don't stop or they'll get you!

She can hear their voices behind her. It's hard to run when your feet are tied together. They're faster than she is, even though they are just walking.

"Oh, Holly," one of them yells. "Hoooolllllyyy!"

Holly pants, trying to push herself forward. She wants desperately to move faster, but the rope tied around her feet blocks them and she falls flat on her face onto the asphalt. Holly screams loudly as her nose scratches across the ground.

Get up! Get up and run. You can't let them get you.

She can hear them laughing behind her.

You can make it, Holly. Just get to A1A right in front of you. Only about a hundred feet left. There are cars on the road. They'll see you. Someone will see you and help you.

She tries to scream, but she has no air in her lungs. She is exhausted from swimming with her legs tied together. Luckily, her arms got free when she jumped in the water. They have pulled off her pants. Cut them open with a knife and pulled them off. Before they stabbed her in the shoulder. It hurts when she runs. Blood has soaked her white shirt. She is naked from the stomach down, except for her shoes and socks. Holly is in so much pain and can hardly move. Yet, she fights to get closer to the road.

A car drives by. Then another one. She can see them in the distance, yet her vision is getting foggier. She can't lose consciousness now.

You've got to keep fighting. You've got to get out of here! Don't give up, Holly. Whatever you do, just don't give up.

Their footsteps are approaching from behind. Holly is groaning and fighting to get a few more steps in.

So close now. So close.

"Hurry up," she hears them yell. "She's getting away!"

Holly is so close now she can smell the cars' exhaust. All she needs to do is get onto the road, then stop a car. That's all she needs to do to get out of there alive. And she is so close now.

"Stop her, goddammit," a voice yells.

Holly fights to run. She moves her feet faster than she feels is humanly possible. She is getting there. She is getting there. She can hear them start to run now. They are yelling to each other.

"Shoot her, dammit."

Holly gasps, thinking about the spear gun. She's the one who taught them how to shoot it. She knows they won't hesitate to use it to stop her. She knows how they think. She knows this is what they do. She knows this is a kick for them, a drug.

She knows, because she is one of them.

"Stop the bitch!" someone yells, and she hears the sound of the gun going off. She knows this sound so well, having been spearfishing all her life and practiced using the gun on land with her father. He taught her everything about spearfishing, starting when she was no more than four years old. He even taught her to hold her breath underwater for a very long time.

"Scuba diving is for tourists. Real fishers free dive," she hears his voice say, the second the spear whistles through the air.

It hits Holly in the leg and she tumbles to the ground. Holly falls to the pavement next to A1A with a scream. She hears giggles and voices behind her. But she can also hear something else. While she drags herself across the pavement, she can hear the sound of sirens.

"Shit!" the voices behind her say.

"We gotta get out of here."

"RUN!"

1

SEPTEMBER 2015

BLAKE MILLS IS ENJOYING his coffee at Starbucks. He enjoys it especially today. He is sipping it while looking at his own painting that they have just put up on display inside the shop. He has been trying to convince the owner of the local Starbucks in Cocoa Beach for ages to put up some of his art on display, and finally Ray agreed to let him hang up one of his turtle paintings. Just for a short period, to see how it goes.

It is Blake's personal favorite painting and he hopes it will attract some business his way. As a small artist in a small town, it is hard to make a living, even though Blake offers paintings by order, so anyone can get one any way they want it and can be sure it will fit their house or condo. It isn't exactly the way the life of an artist is supposed to be, but it is the only way to do it if he wants to eat.

Blake decides to make it a day of celebration and buys an extra coffee and a piece of cake to eat as well. He takes a bite and enjoys the taste.

"Looking good," a voice says behind him. He turns in his chair and looks into the eyes of Olivia.

Olivia Hartman. The love of his life.

Blake smiles to himself. "You came," he whispers and looks around. Being married, Olivia has to be careful whom she is seen with in this town.

"Can I sit?" she asks, holding her own coffee in her hand.

Blake pulls out a chair for her and she sits next to him. Blake feels a big thrill run through his body. He loves being with Olivia and has never had the pleasure of doing so in public. They usually meet up at his studio and have sex between his paintings on the floor or up against the wall. He has never been to her place on Patrick Air Force Base, where she lives with her husband, a general in the army. Blake is terrified of him and a little of her as well, but that is part of what makes it so wonderfully exciting. At the age of twenty-three, Blake isn't ready to settle down with anyone, and he isn't sure he is ever going to be. It isn't his style. He likes the carefree life, and being an artist he can't exactly provide for a family anyway. Having children will only force him to forget his dreams and get a *real job*. It would no doubt please his father, but Blake doesn't want a real job. He doesn't want the house on the water or the two to three children. He isn't cut out for it, and his many girlfriends in the past never understood that. All of them thought they could change him, that they were the one who could make him realize that he wanted it all. But he really didn't. And he still doesn't.

"It looks really great," Olivia says and sips her coffee. She is wearing multiple finger rings and bracelets, as always. She is delicate, yet strong. Used to be a fighter pilot in the army. Blake thought that was so cool. Today, she no longer works, not since she married the general.

She and Blake had met at the Officer's Club across the street from the base. He was there with a girl he had met at Grills in Cape Canaveral, who worked on base doing some contracting or something boring like that; she had invited him to a party. It was by far the most boring affair until he met Olivia on the porch standing with a beer in her hand overlooking the Atlantic Ocean. She was slightly tipsy and they exchanged pleasantries for a few minutes before she turned and looked at him with that mischievous smile of hers. Then she asked him if he wanted to have some fun.

"Always," he replied.

They walked to the beach and into the dunes, where they enjoyed the best sex of Blake's life.

Now it has become a drug to him. He needs his fix. He needs her.

"Congrats," she says.

"Thanks. Now I just hope someone will grab one of the business cards I've put on the counter and call me to order a painting. I could use the money. I only had one order last month."

"They will," she says, laughing. "Don't you worry about that." She leans over and whispers through those pouty lips of hers. "Now let's go back to your place and celebrate."

"Is that an order?" he asks, laughing.

"Is that an order, *ma'am*," she corrects him. "And, yes, it is."

2

SEPTEMBER 2015

Being with Olivia is exhilarating. It fills him with the most wonderful sensation in his body because Blake has never met anyone like her, who can make him crazy for her. Not like this. But at the same time, it is also absolutely petrifying because she is married to General Hartman, who will have Blake killed if he ever finds out. There is no doubt about it in Blake's mind.

Yet, he keeps sleeping with her. Even though he keeps telling himself it is a bad idea, that he has to stop, that it is only a matter of time before he will get himself in some deep shit trouble. Blake knows it is bad to be with her. He knows it will get him in trouble eventually, but still, he can't help himself. He has to have her. He has to taste her again and again. No matter the cost.

Their lips meet inside Blake's studio as soon as they walk in. Blake closes his eyes and drinks from her. He doesn't care that the door behind him is left open. Nothing else matters right now.

"I thought you couldn't get out today," he says, panting, when her lips leave his. "Isn't the general on base?"

"He is," she mumbles between more kisses.

It has been two weeks since they were together last. Two weeks of constantly dreaming and longing for her. They communicate via Snapchat. It is untraceable, as far as Blake knows. Blake wrote a message to her a few days ago, telling her about the painting being put up in Starbucks, knowing that she probably couldn't come and see it. He even sent a picture of the painting. It is also her favorite. She messaged him back a photo of her sad face telling him she didn't think she could get out, since her husband was home. Usually, she only dares to meet with Blake when her husband is travelling. Even then, they have to be extremely careful. General Hartman has many friends in Cocoa Beach and his soldiers are seen everywhere.

"I told him I was seeing a friend today. It's not like it's a lie. I don't care anymore if he finds out about us. I'm sick of being just the general's wife. I want a life of my own."

Blake takes off his T-shirt and her hands land on his chest. He rips off her shirt and several buttons fall to the floor. She closes her eyes and moans at his touches. His hands cup her breasts and soon her bra lands on the wooden floor. He grabs her hair and pulls her head back while kissing her neck. His heart is pumping in his chest just from the smell of her skin.

"You can't," he whispers between breaths. "You can't let him know about us. He'll kill the both of us."

Olivia lets out a gasp as Blake reaches up under her skirt and places a hand in her panties, and then rips them off. He pushes her up against a table, then lifts her up, leans over her naked torso and puts his mouth to her breasts. He closes his eyes and takes in her smell, drinking the juices of her body, then pulls his shorts down and gently slides inside of her with a deep moan. She puts her legs around his neck, partly strangling him when she comes in pulsing movements back and forth, her body arching.

"Oh, Blake…oh, Blake …"

The sensation is burning inside of him and he is ready to explode. Olivia is moaning and moving rapidly. His movements are urgent now, the intensity building. He is about to burst, when suddenly she screams loudly and pushes him away. Blake falls to the floor with a thud.

"What the…?"

Blake soon realizes why Olivia is screaming and feels the blood rush from his face. A set of eyes is staring down at him.

The eyes of Detective Chris Fisher.

"Blake Mills, you're under arrest," the voice belonging to the eyes says.

3

SEPTEMBER 2015

"I'm sorry, Mary, there's nothing I can do."

I stare at my boss, Chief Editor, Markus Fergusson. He is leaning back in his leather chair in his office on the twenty-eighth floor of the Times-Tower on the west side of midtown. Behind him, the view is spectacular, but I hardly notice anymore. After five years working there, you simply stop being baffled. However, I am actually baffled at this moment. But not because of the view. Because of what is being said.

"So, you're firing me, is that it?" I ask, while my blood is boiling in my veins. What the hell is this?

"We're letting you go, yes."

"You can't do that, Markus, come on. Just because of this?"

He leans over his desk and gives me that look that I have come to know so well in my five years as a reporter for *The New York Times*.

"Yes."

"I don't get it," I say. "I'm being fired for writing the paper's most read article in the past five years?"

Markus sighs. "Don't put up a fight, will you? Just accept it. You violated the rules, sweetheart."

Don't you sweetheart me, you pig!

"I don't make the rules, Mary. The big guys upstairs make the decisions and it says here that we have to let you go for *violating the normal editing process.*"

I squint my eyes. I can't believe this. "I did what?"

"You printed the story without having a second set of eyes on it first. The article offended some people, and, well…"

He pauses. I scoff. He is such a sell-out. Just because my article didn't sit well with some people, some influential people, he is letting me go? They want to fire me for some rule bullshit?

"Brian saw it," I say. "He read it and approved it."

"The rules say *two* editors," he says. "On a story like this, this controversial, you need two editors to approve it, not just one."

"That's BS and you know it, goddammit, Markus. I never even heard about this rule. What about Brian?"

"We're letting him go as well."

"You can't do that! The man just had another kid."

Markus shrugs. "That's not really my problem, is it? Brian knew better. He's been with us for fifteen years."

"It was late, Markus. We had less than five minutes to deadline. There was no time to get another approval. If we'd waited for another editor, the story wouldn't have run, and you wouldn't have sold a record number of newspapers that day. The article went viral online. All over the world. Everyone was talking about it. And this is how you thank me?"

I rise from the chair and grab my leather jacket. "Well, suit yourself. It's your loss. I don't need you or this paper."

I leave, slamming the door, but it doesn't make me feel as good as I thought it would. I pack my things in that little brown box that they always do in the movies and grab it under my arm before I leave in the elevator. On the bottom floor, I hand in my ID card to the guard in the lobby and Johnson looks at me with his mouth turned downwards.

"We'll miss you, Miss Mary," he says.

"I'll miss you too, Johnson," I say, and walk out the glass doors, into the streets of New York without a clue as to what I am going to do. Living in Manhattan isn't cheap. Living in Manhattan with a nine-year old son, as a single mom isn't cheap at all. The cost for a private school alone is over the roof.

I whistle for a cab, and before I finally get one, it starts to rain, and I get soaked. I have him drive me back to my apartment and I let myself inside. Snowflake, my white Goldendoodle is waiting on the other side of the door, jumping me when I enter. He licks me in my face and whimpers from having missed me since I left just this morning. I sit down on my knees and pet him till he calms down. I can't help smiling when I am with him. I can't feel sad for long when he's around. It's simply not possible. He looks at me with those deep brown eyes.

"We'll be alright, won't we, Snowflake? I'm sure we will. We don't need them, no we don't."

4

SEPTEMBER 2015

"Do you come here often?"

Liz Hester stares at the man who has approached her in the bar at Lou's Blues in Indialantic. It is Friday night and she was bored at the base, so she and her friends decided to go out and get a beer.

"You're kidding me, right?"

The guy smiles. He is a surfer-type with long greasy hair under his cap, a nice tan, and not too much between the ears. The kind of guy who opens each sentence with *dude,* even when speaking to a girl.

"It was the best I could come up with."

"You do realize that I am thirty-eight and you're at least fifteen years younger, right?"

Kim comes up behind her. She is wearing her blue ASU— army service uniform—like Liz. They are both decorated with several medals. Liz's includes the Purple Heart, given to her when she was shot during her service in Afghanistan. Took a bullet straight to her shoulder. The best part was, she took it for one of her friends. She took it for Britney, who is also with them this night, hanging out with some guy further down the bar. They are friends through thick and thin. Will lay down their lives for one another.

Liz's eyes meet those of Jamie's across the bar. She smiles and nods in the direction of the guy that Liz is talking to. Liz smiles and nods too. There is no need for them to speak; they know what she is saying.

He's the one.

"So, tell me, what's your name?" Liz asks the guy. She is all of a sudden flirtatious, smiling and touching his arm gently. Kim giggles behind her, but the guy doesn't notice.

"I'm Billy. My friends call me Billy the Kid."

"Well, you are just a kid, aren't you?" she says, purring like a cat, leaning in over the bar.

The guy lifts his cap a little, then puts it back on. "You sure are a lot of woman."

Liz knows his type. He is one of those who gets aroused just by looking at a woman in uniform. She has met her share of those types. They are a lot of fun to play with.

"Well, maybe I can make a man of you," she whispers, leaning very close to his face.

The guy laughs goofily. "You sure can," he says and gives her an elevator look. "I sure wouldn't mind that. I got an anaconda in my pants you can ride if you like."

Liz laughs lightly, and then looks at Jamie again, letting her know he has taken the bait.

"Well, why don't you—Billy the Kid—meet me outside in the parking lot in say—five minutes?"

Billy laughs again. "Dude! Whoa, sure!"

Billy taps the bar counter twice, not knowing exactly what to do with himself, then lifts his cap once again and wipes sweat off his forehead. He has nice eyes, Liz thinks, and he is quite handsome.

As stupid as they get, though.

He leaves her, shooting a finger-gun at her and winking at

the same time. The girls approach Liz, moving like cats sliding across the floor. Liz finishes her drink while the four of them stick their heads together.

"Ready for some fun?" she asks.

They don't say anything. They don't have to.

5

SEPTEMBER 2015

SHE WAITS for him by the car. Smoking a cigarette, she leans against it, blowing out smoke when she spots him come out of the bar and walk towards her. Seeing the goofy grin on his face makes her smile even wider.

"Hey there, baby," Billy says and walks up to her. "I have to say, I wasn't sure you would even be here. A nice lady like you with a guy like me? You're a wild cat, aren't you?"

Liz chuckles and blows smoke in his face. "I sure am."

Billy the Kid moves his body in anticipation. His crotch can't keep still. He is already hard.

What a sucker.

He looks around with a sniffle. "So, where do you want to go? To the beach? Or do you...wanna do it right here...?" he places a hand next to her on the car. "Up against this baby, huh?"

Liz laughs again, then leans closer to him till her mouth is on his ear. "You're just full of yourself, aren't you?"

"What?" he asks with another goofy grin.

"Did you really think you were going to get lucky with me? With this?" She says and points up and down her body.

The grin is wiped off his face. Finally.

"What is this?" he asks, his face in a frown. "Were you just leading me on? What a cunt!" He spits out the last word. He probably means it as an insult, but Liz just smiles from ear to ear as her friends slowly approach from all sides, surrounding Billy. When he realizes, he tries to back out, but walks into Jamie and steps on her black shoes.

"Hey, those are brand new! Dammit!"

Jamie pushes him in the back forcefully and he is now in the hands of Britney. Britney is smaller than the others, but by far the strongest. She clenches her fist and slams it into his face. The blow breaks his nose on the spot and he falls backwards to the asphalt, blood running from it.

"What the…what…who are you?" Billy asks, disoriented, looking from woman to woman.

"We like to call ourselves the Fast and the Furious," Liz says.

"Yeah, cause I'm fast," Kim says and kicks Billy in the crotch. He lets out a loud moan in pain.

The sound is almost arousing to Liz.

"And I'm furious," she says, grabbing him by the hair and pulling his head back. She looks him in the eyes. She loves watching them squirm, the little suckers. Just like she loved it back in Afghan when she interrogated the *Haji*.

Haji is the name they call anyone of Arab decent, or even of a brownish skin tone. She remembers vividly the first time they brought one in. It was the day after she had lost a good friend to an IED, a roadside bomb that detonated and killed everyone in the truck in front of her. They searched for those suckers all night, and finally, the next morning they brought in three. Boy, she kicked that sucker till he could no longer move. Hell, they all did it. All of them let out their frustrations. Losing three good soldiers like that made them furious.

Liz was still furious. Well, to be frank, she has been furious all of her life.

Everybody around her knows that.

Liz laughs when she hears Billy's whimper, then uses two fingers to poke his eyes forcefully. Billy screams.

"My eyes, my eyes!"

Liz lets go of his hair and looks at her girls. They are all about to burst in anticipation. She opens the door to the car, where Jamie has placed a couple of bottles of vodka to keep them going all night. She lets out a loud howl like a wolf, the girls chiming in, then lifts Billy the Kid up and throws him in the back of the Jeep.

6

FEBRUARY 1977

WHEN PENELOPE and Peter get married, she is already showing. It is no longer a secret to the people at the wedding, even though her mother does all she can to disguise it by buying a big dress. By the time of the wedding, Penelope has grown into it and her stomach fills it out completely. Peter's mother tells her she looks radiant and gorgeous, but Penelope's own mother hates the fact that people will talk about the marriage as a necessity, or *the right thing to do,* and their daughter as only getting married because she is pregnant. Because she has to.

But that is just the way it is, and no one cares less about what people think than Penelope and Peter. They are happy and looking forward to becoming parents more than anything.

Soon after the wedding, the bank approves a loan for them and they buy their dream house in Cocoa Beach. As a young lawyer who has just been made partner, Peter is doing well, and even though it is one of the most expensive locations in Cocoa Beach, Penelope doesn't have to work anymore. She quits her job as a secretary and wants to focus on her family and later charity work. It is the kind of life they have both dreamed of, and no one is more thrilled to see it come true than Penelope.

"I can't wait to become a family," she says, when Peter is done fixing up the nursery and shows it to her.

Seeing how beautiful he has decorated it makes her cry, and she holds a hand to her ready-to-burst stomach. Only two more weeks till she will hold her baby. Only two more weeks.

She can hardly wait.

Peter is going to be a wonderful father; she just knows he will. He has such a kind and gentle personality. She has done right in choosing him. She knows she has. This is going to be a perfect little family. Penelope already knows she wants lots of children. At least two, maximum four. She herself comes from a family of four children. Four girls, to be exact. There was a brother, but he died at an early age after a long illness. Being the oldest, Penelope took care of him, and it was devastating for her when he passed away. It is a sorrow she can never get rid of, and often she blames herself for not being able to cure him. Later in life, she played with the idea of becoming a doctor, but she never had the grades for it.

Peter, on the other hand, is an only child. His mother has spoiled his socks off all of his life. She still does every now and then. And she still treats him like a child sometimes. It makes Penelope laugh out loud when she spit-washes him or corrects his tie. But she is nice, Peter's mom. She has always loved Penelope, and there is nothing bad to be said about her.

It was always the plan that Peter would follow in his father's footsteps and go to law school, and so he did. He met Penelope right after he passed the bar and started working at the small law firm in Rockledge where she was a secretary. Soon he moved on to a bigger firm and now he had made partner.

Peter's career exploded within a few years, and now he is talking about going into real estate as well. He has so many plans for their future, and she knows he will always take care of them. She is never going to want for anything.

Two weeks later, her water breaks. Penelope is standing in the kitchen admiring the new tiles they have put in, with a coffee cup in her hand. The water soaks her dress and the floor beneath her. Penelope gasps and reaches for the phone. She calls Peter at the office.

"This is it," she says, with a mixture of excitement and fright in her voice. "Our baby is coming, Peter. Our baby is coming!"

"I…I'll be right there."

Peter stumbles over himself on his way out of the office and the secretary has to yell at him to come back because he has forgotten his car keys.

Peter rushes her to the hospital, where the contractions soon take over and after a tough struggle and fourteen hours of labor, she is finally holding her baby girl in her arms.

"Look at her, Peter," she says through tears. "I…I simply can't stop looking at her. I am so happy, Peter. You made me so happy, thank you. Thank you so much."

7

SEPTEMBER 2015

I SPEND the evening feeling sorry for myself. I cook chicken in green curry, my favorite dish these days, and sulk in front of the TV watching back-to-back episodes of *Friends* with Snowflake and my son Salter next to me.

"They can't fire you!" Salter exclaimed, when I told him as soon as he got home from school. He knew something was wrong as soon as he saw that I'd made hot cocoa for the both of us and put marshmallows in it.

That is kind of my thing. Whenever I have bad news, I prepare hot cocoa with marshmallows. I have also baked cookies. That is another diversion of mine. Nothing keeps me as distracted as baking or cooking.

"You're the best damn reporter they have!"

"I am, but there's no need to curse," I say.

I enjoy spending the rest of the evening with the loves of my life, both of them, and decide to not wonder about my future until the next day. Salter is so loving and caring towards me and keeps asking me if there is anything he can do for me, to make me feel better.

"Just stay here in my arms," I say and pull him closer.

He has reached the age where he still enjoys my affectionate hugs and holding him close, but lately he has begun to find them annoying from time to time, especially when it is in front of his friends.

I named him Salter because I have been a surfer all of my life, growing up in Cocoa Beach, and so is his dad. Salter means *derived from salt*. We believed he was born of our love for the ocean. How foolish and young we were back then.

It feels like a lifetime ago.

"So, what do we do now?" Salter finally asks when the episode where Phoebe fights with a fire alarm is over.

I take in a deep breath. I know he has to wonder. I do too, but I try not to think about it. Mostly to make sure he isn't affected by it.

"I mean, now that you don't have a job?" he continues. "Can we still live in this apartment?"

"I have to be honest with you, kiddo," I say. "I don't know. I don't know what is going to happen. I am not sure any newspaper will have me after this. I pissed off some pretty influential people."

"That's stupid," he says. "They're all stupid. Your article had more views than anyone's."

"I know, but that isn't always enough, buddy."

I sigh, hoping I don't have to go into details, when suddenly my phone rings. I let go of Salter and lean over to pick it up from the coffee table. My heart drops when I see the name on the display.

It's my dad.

"It's Mary," I say, my heart throbbing in my throat. I haven't spoken to my dad in at least a year. He never calls me.

"Mary." His voice is heavy. Something is definitely going on.

"What's wrong, Dad? Are you sick?"

"No. It's not me. It's your brother."

I swallow hard. My brother is the only family member I still have regular contact with. I love the little bastard, even if he is fifteen years younger than me.

"Blake? What's wrong with him?"

"It's bad, Mary. He's been arrested."

Arrested?!?

"What? Why…for what…what's going on, Dad?"

My father sighs from the other end of the line. "For murder. He's been arrested for murder."

8

SEPTEMBER 2015

THEY TAKE HIM FOR A RIDE. Billy the Kid is crying in the back when the girls take him first to the Super Wal-Mart in Merritt Island that is open 24/7. Placing a knife to his back, they walk through the store and pull bottles of wine, gin, and tequila from the shelves. They even find a fishing pole that they think could be fun to buy. Along with some chips Jamie wants, and sugarcoated donuts. Kim has a craving for cheesecake while Britney wants chocolate. And loads of it. Liz holds the knife in Billy's back and asks them to throw in some Choco-mint ice cream for her. Then she grabs a bottle of drain cleaner. They tell Billy to take out his wallet and pay for everything.

"If you as much as whimper, I will split you open," Liz whispers, as they come closer to the cashier. "I'll make it look like you attacked me. Who do you think they'll believe, huh? A surfer dude or a decorated war-veteran? A female one on top of it."

After he pays, they open a bottle of gin and take turns drinking from it while they drive, screaming and cheering, back to Cocoa Beach where they park in front of Ron Jon's surf-shop, which is also open 24/7. Yelling and visibly intoxicated, they storm inside with Billy and take the elevator to the second floor. They run through the aisles of bikinis and pull down one after another.

"I always wanted yellow one," Kim yells.

"I'm going red this time," Britney says. "Wouldn't this look cute on me?"

"Grab me one of the striped ones over there," Liz says. "Size medium."

Kim giggles cheerfully then grabs one. They don't bother to try them on. There is no time for that. Kim also grabs a couple of nice shirts from Billabong, and then some shorts from Roxy for Liz.

"Oh," Britney says and points at the surfboards on the other side of the store. She looks to the others. "I always wanted a surfboard!"

"Me too," Jamie exclaims. "Let's find one!"

"I...I can't afford that," Billy whimpers. "Aren't they like four hundred dollars?"

"This one is five hundred dollars," Jamie says, and looks at a seven-foot fun-shape. "Doesn't it look GREAT on me?"

"Adorable," Liz says and laughs.

"I can't afford this," Billy whimpers over and over when they pull the boards out.

"Grab one for me too," Liz says, ignoring his complaints. She presses the knife into his back, puts her arm around his neck, then kisses his cheek, making it look like they are a couple.

"You'll have to," she whispers. "I'll make a scene. Make it look like you tried to rape me."

"Okay, okay," he says with a moan. "Just don't hurt me, okay? Just let me go after this, alright?"

She doesn't make any promises. That's not how Liz rolls.

They charge everything to one of Billy's credit cards, then run out of the store carrying surfboards and plastic bags with bikinis, hollering and laughing. They throw everything in the car and strap the boards onto the roof before driving to the International Palms Resort a few blocks further down A1A, where they book a suite for all of them, charging it on his credit card again.

"Please don't make me pay for any more," he says in the elevator.

They ignore his complaints, and then storm into the room. It is huge and has great views of the ocean. Liz lets go of Billy, then throws him on the white couch. Jamie grabs one of the bottles of Vodka and places it to her lips. She drinks it like it is water. Liz laughs and pulls the bottle from Jamie's hand. She places it to her lips and closes her eyes while it burns its way down her throat.

"Hey, leave some for the rest of us," Kim yells, and grabs the bottle out of Liz's hand.

The vodka spills on Liz's white shirt. Liz looks angrily at Kim. "What the hell…?"

Kim laughs, then drinks from the bottle. Liz clenches her fist before she slams it into Kim's face as soon as she lets go of the bottle again. Kim falls backwards, then stares, confused, at Liz.

"What…what happened?" she asks.

Liz grabs the bottle out of her hand forcefully. Jamie and Britney remain quiet. They dare not make a sound. The feeling of power intoxicates Liz. Liz looks at Billy the Kid, who is squirming on the couch while staring at them with terror in his eyes.

Liz approaches him. He squirms again. Liz leans over and kisses him forcefully. He tries to push her away, but two of the other girls grab his arms and hold him down while Liz has her way with him. She pulls off his pants and then she laughs.

"Is that all? Is that the anaconda you wanted me to ride?"

"Please, just let me go," Billy says, crying in humiliation

"I've done everything you wanted me to. I've paid for everything. Please, just let me go."

"Now he wants to leave. You finally have the chance to get laid and now you want to leave? No no, Billy, tsk tsk. That's not what a woman wants to hear, is it, girls?"

The three others shake their heads.

Liz puts her hand on his penis and starts to rub. Soon, his anaconda grows sizably and he starts moaning.

"Please...please..."

She puts her lips on it and makes him hard, then sits on top of him and rides him. The other girls are screaming with joy. Liz rides him forcefully, and soon they both come with deep moans.

Liz smiles when Billy arches in spasms and she feels his semen inside of her, then leans over and kisses his forehead.

"If you tell the police what we did tonight, I'll tell them you raped me," she whispers. "That you were holding a gun to my head and you raped me. Boy, I do believe I even have three witnesses. Three VERY reliable witnesses."

Liz finishes with a laugh, then climbs off Billy. "Come on girls," she says. "Let's get *really* drunk."

She grabs a bottle and drinks from it. It is strange how it feels like she can't get drunk anymore. Not like *really* drunk. Not like in the old days. Liz likes being really drunk. It makes her forget. It is the only thing that can make her forget.

The girls throw themselves at the chips and candy they bought at Wal-Mart. Liz looks at them with contempt. They have no self-control, these girls. Kim buries her hands in the cheesecake and eats it, licking her fingers. Jamie stuffs her face with donuts and has sugar all over her mouth.

Liz sighs.

"You want some ice cream?" Jamie asks.

"I don't want some stupid ice cream," Liz says, mocking

Jamie. "I'm bored." She looks at Billy, who doesn't dare to move on the couch. "He bores me."

"What do you want to do?" Kim asks.

"Yeah, do you want to have another go?" Jamie asks.

Liz throws the bottle in her hand against the wall. It breaks and leaves a huge mark that Billy is probably going to pay for. Liz growls and kicks the ice cream bucket.

"I'm sick of the prick. He's no fun to play with."

Liz grabs the drain cleaner and walks towards Billy with firm steps. The girls all look at her. Serious eyes follow her every step. The atmosphere in the room immediately changes. No one is laughing anymore. No one is eating.

"What are you doing with that, babe?" Jamie asks.

"Don't do it," Kim yells.

But Liz doesn't listen. She opens the lid and grabs Billy's jaw. She forces it open. Billy is squirming too much and she can't do it on her own.

"Help me, dammit," she yells.

The girls hesitate, but don't dare not to do as they're told. Who knows what Liz might do next? Who will be next? They have seen too much to be able to say no.

Britney is first to grab Billy's right arm and hold it down. Jamie then grabs the left one. Kim holds his head still, while Liz pours the liquid drain cleaner into his mouth and down his throat. The three girls stare at her while she empties the bottle completely. They dare not even to speak. Billy's screams pierce through their bones. No one dares to move.

Liz throws the empty bottle on the ground, then looks at her friends. "Let's get out of here," she yells.

Her words are almost drowned out by Billy's scream.

9

SEPTEMBER 2015

I LAND at Orlando airport around noon the next day. Salter and Snowflake are both with me. We have packed two big suitcases, not knowing how long we are going to stay. My dad tried to convince me there is no need for me to come down, but I didn't listen. I need to be there. I need to help my brother.

"What about my school?" Salter says, as we walk to the rental car.

"I called them and told them it's a family emergency," I say. "They told me you have to be back in ten days or your spot goes to someone else. They mean business, that school."

It is one of the best schools in New York and one of the most expensive ones too. I haven't decided if I like it or not. The uniforms I can do without, but that kind of comes with the territory. It is mostly the way they shape them into small soldiers there, always running all these tests, making them stand straight, and never having time to play. It is all Salter knows, so to him, it is fine. But there is something about the school that I don't like. I find it hard to enjoy that my child is going to a school like this. Joey and I are both surfers and free spirits. This school is not us at all. Yet, we signed Salter up for it as soon as we moved to New York.

We moved because of my job, but unfortunately it turned out to be the end of our little family. Joey had nothing to do up there, since no one would hire him, and soon we grew apart. Staying at home and not having anything to do wore on him. He never felt like he accomplished anything or that he was supporting his family, and that is important to him. He started to feel lonely and sought comfort in the arms of a young girl who worked at a small coffee house on our street. He would go there every day to drink his coffee and write. He wants to be an author and has written several books, but no publisher will touch them. I think they are beautiful and inspiring, but I guess I am biased. I love Joey. I still do. But when he told me he had slept with the girl at the coffee house several times a week for at least a year, I threw him out. Well, not right away. First, I gave him a second chance and we tried to make it work for a couple of weeks, for Salter's sake, but I couldn't stand thinking about it all day, whether he'd been with her again. It tore me apart. I have never been a jealous person, but this I couldn't handle. I tried hard to, but realized I wasn't as forgiving as I thought I could be. I didn't have it in me and I felt like I could never trust him again. So, I finally asked him to move out.

"Where do you want me to go?" he asked.

I shrugged. "Go live with that coffee house girl. I don't know."

He decided to go back to Cocoa Beach where we grew up together. That was four months ago now. I miss him every day. But I can't forget what he did. What hurts the most is the betrayal, the deceit. I don't know how to move past it. I don't know if I ever can.

He calls as often as he can and talks to Salter. It's been hard on our son. He loves his dad and needs him in his life, needs a male role model. Salter went to visit him during summer break, and it is the plan that he will be going down for Thanksgiving as well.

"You think I can call Dad now?" Salter asks, as soon as we are in the car and hit the beach line.

I sigh. It is such a big blow to Salter that his dad moved this far away. I know he is excited to see him again. I hate to see that look in his eyes. He doesn't know his dad cheated on me. He only knows that he left, and that is enough. I know he feels guilt and questions if he had something to do with it. I try to tell him it wasn't because of him, that sometimes grown-ups grow apart, that they can't make it work anymore. I am not sure he is convinced.

"Sure," I say.

Salter smiles and grabs my phone and finds his dad's number. While driving towards the beach and listening to him talk to his father, I feel a chill go through my body. I watch the big signs for Ron Jon's surf shop go by and realize my hands are shivering. Everything about this place gives me the creeps. I haven't been back in almost twenty years. Not since I left for college.

Blake was three years old back then. Joey and I have lived all over since. He worked with whatever he could get his hands on, mostly as a carpenter. I spent five years working for CNN in Atlanta, which became my biggest career jump. Before that I held a position with *USA Today* in Virginia. I started my career as a journalist at *Miami Herald* and we lived for a while in Ft. Lauderdale before my job took us out of the state, something I had dreamed of as long as I could remember. To get away.

Salter puts the phone down.

"So, what did he have to say?" I ask, as we approach the bridges that will take us to the Barrier Islands. In the distance, I can see the cruise ships. A sign tells me I can go on a casino cruise for free. Gosh, how I hate this place…with all its tourists and tiki bars.

"He can't wait to see me," Salter says.

I turn onto A1A, where all the condominiums and hotels are lined up like pearls on a string.

"At least you'll have fun seeing your dad," I say, while wondering what is waiting for me once I arrive at my childhood home. What is it going to be like to see my dad again? What about Blake? I haven't seen him in several years. He visited me in New York five years ago, but other than that, we have mainly spoken over the phone or on Facebook. We aren't very close, but he is still the only one in my family I like. He is all the family I have, and I will do anything to help him out.

Anything.

10

APRIL 1977

PENELOPE AND PETER take the baby home to their new house a few days after the birth. In the months to follow, they try everything they can to become a family. But the sleep deprivation is hard on them. Especially on Penelope. She gets up four or sometimes five times a night to breastfeed, and all day long she feels sick from the lack of sleep.

Only a few weeks after the baby arrived Peter gets a new case. It is a big deal, he explains to Penelope, one of those cases that can make or break a career. And Peter is determined to make it.

But that means long days at the office, and Penelope is soon alone for many hours at the house. Sometimes, he even stays away the entire night just to work, and when he finally comes home, he is too worn out to even speak to his wife.

Penelope, on the other hand, longs to speak with an adult and can hardly stop talking to him and asking him questions.

"How was your day? What's the latest on the case? Do you think you'll be done in time?"

Peter answers with a growl and tries to avoid her. As soon as he comes home, he storms to the restroom and stays in there for at least an hour, reading a magazine or the newspaper just to get a little peace and quiet.

The first weeks, Penelope waits outside the door and attacks him with more questions or demands as soon as he pokes his head out again.

"The garage door is acting up again. Could you fix it or call someone who could? We need to start thinking about preschool. I've looked over a few of them, but I need your help to choose the right one. What do you think? I was thinking about painting the living room another color. A light blue, maybe?"

One day he comes home at nine in the evening after a very stressful day and all he dreams of is throwing himself on the couch, putting his feet up, and reading the newspaper, enjoying a nice quiet evening. When he enters the house, Penelope comes down from upstairs holding the baby in her arms with a deep sigh. The look in her eyes is of complete desperation.

"Where have you been?"

He sighs and closes the front door behind him. He doesn't have the energy to explain to her what's been going on at the office.

"A long story," he says, and puts his briefcase down.

The baby wails. Penelope looks at her with concern. "No. No. Not again. Please don't start again." She looks at Peter. "She's been like this all day, Peter. I don't know what to do. I don't know anymore. I just really, really need time…just an hour of sleep. I'm so tired."

Peter looks at her. Is she kidding him?

"We're both tired," he says.

"No. No. It's more than that, Peter. She's driving me nuts. It's like torture. I can't eat. I can't think. I can't…"

"Could you shut up for just one second?"

Penelope stares at her husband. "Excuse me?"

"Do you have ANY idea what kind of day I've had? Do you have ANY idea what I am going through these days? I think you can manage a little crying baby, all right? I would give anything to be in your shoes and not have to deal with this case."

Peter snorts, then walks past her into the living room, where he closes the door. Penelope has a lump in her throat. She feels so helpless. So alone and so so incredibly tired. She looks at the baby, who is still crying.

"Why are you crying little baby, huh? Why are you crying so much?"

She puts her lips on the baby's forehead to kiss her, but the kiss makes her realize something. Something she should have noticed a long time ago. The baby isn't just fussing.

She is burning up with a fever.

11

SEPTEMBER 2015

I DRIVE into the driveway at 701 S Atlantic Avenue and park in front of the garage. I turn off the engine with a deep sigh. Everything looks the same from the outside. Same brown garage doors, even though the painting needs to be redone, same lawn in front and same old palm tree, even though it is a lot taller. The bushes to the right have been removed and new flowers have been planted. I know nothing about plants or flowers, but these are orange and look stunning.

"How come we have never visited granddad before?" my son asks.

I look at him. I knew the question had to come at some point. But I am not ready to provide the answer.

"Let's go in," I say.

We grab our suitcases and drag them across the bricks towards the entrance to my dad's beach house, my childhood home. I can smell the ocean from the behind the house. I close my eyes and breathe it in. So many memories, good and bad, are combined with this smell. I love the ocean. I still do. Joey and I both love it and spent so many hours surfing together while growing up.

But there is also all the bad stuff. The stuff I haven't talked about since I left town for college at age eighteen. The stuff I had hoped I never would have to talk about again. Ever.

Just before we reach the front door, I turn my head and look down at 7th Street behind me, on the other side of Atlantic Avenue or A1A as we call it. 7th street continues all the way down to the Intracoastal Waters, or Banana River, and in most of those houses had lived kids. I had known all of them. We used to be a tight bunch of seven children. All of us went to Roosevelt Elementary and later Cocoa Beach High School. We used to bicycle to school together and after school we would rush back to check out the surf from the crosswalk on 7th, then grab our boards if the waves were good and surf for hours. We used to call ourselves *The 7th Street Crew*. I was the rich kid among them, with the biggest house on the ocean with a pool and guesthouse. But I was never the happiest.

"Mary!"

The face in the doorway belongs to my dad's girlfriend, Laura. We don't like her. She came into our lives two years before I left home, so I had the privilege of living with her for two very long years before I could finally leave.

"Hi, Laura," I say, forcing a smile.

"Oh…and you brought a dog. How wonderful," she says, staring at Snowflake like he is a vicious monster. Snowflake is anything but that. He is the gentlest dog in the universe, and the fluffiest. He loves children and will run up to anyone simply because he loves people so much. He is white as snow, but has the brownest, deepest puppy-eyes in the world. He is also my best friend in the whole world. He is no guard dog, though. That he cannot do.

"Don't worry," I say. "He doesn't shed. He has poodle in him and they don't shed. He doesn't drool either or bark. He won't be any trouble."

"Well isn't that…nice." Laura speaks through tightened

lips. I know she is going to hate having him here, but I couldn't just leave him in the apartment back home. She will have to live with it.

"And this must be Salter," she says with a gasp. "My gosh, how much you look like your granddad."

"Speaking of...where is the old man?" I ask, feeling uncomfortable already.

"He's in his study. Come in. Come in." Laura makes room for us to enter. Salter goes first.

"Whoa!" he exclaims. "This house is huge." He looks at me like he expects me to have told him about this sooner.

"I put you two in one of the rooms upstairs," Laura says.

"I think we could fit our entire apartment just in this hallway," Salter continues. "Don't you think, Mom?"

"Probably. Now let's get our suitcases to our room, Salter, and then find your granddad."

"I'll let him know you're here," she says. "He hasn't really been himself since...well since Blake...you know."

"He got arrested, Laura. You can say the words. It's not like it's a secret."

"I just didn't want to...in front of the b-o-y."

"He's nine, Laura. He knows how to spell boy. Besides, he knows everything. He can take it."

Laura looks at me like I have no idea how to be a parent. She herself has two daughters of her own that had already moved out when she met my dad. They are a little older than me. I met them once at a Thanksgiving dinner right after Laura moved into our house, and that was no success. Since then, I have passed on all invitations to Thanksgiving and Christmas. After a few years, I think they got the message and stopped asking if we would join them.

"Let me show you to your room." Laura goes ahead of me up the stairs. I am surprised that she hasn't placed me in the guesthouse in the back to keep me out of the house as much as possible, like she did when I was a teenager. As soon as she moved in, I was asked to move to the guesthouse in the back. She wanted to turn my old room into a gym. Back then, I didn't understand why she didn't just chose one of the six other bedrooms in the house, but today I do. She wanted me out and maybe my dad did too. I wasn't exactly an easy teenager. I had a lot of anger built up and was constantly taking it out on him. I blamed him for everything that happened with my mother.

I still do.

END OF EXCERPT...

ORDER YOUR COPY TODAY!

GO HERE TO ORDER:
https://www.amazon.com/What-Hurts-Most-engrossing-heart-stopping-ebook/dp/B018A097LO

Printed in Great Britain
by Amazon